Dunces ROCK

Dunces ROCK

Kate Jaimet

ORCA BOOK PUBLISHERS

Library and Archives Canada Cataloguing in Publication

Jaimet, Kate, 1969-, author
Dunces rock / Kate Jaimet.

Issued in print and electronic formats.
ISBN 978-1-4598-0585-9 (pbk.).--ISBN 978-1-4598-0586-6 (pdf).--
ISBN 978-1-4598-0587-3 (epub)

I. Title.
PS8619.A368D863 2014   jC813'.6   C2014-901584-4
                              C2014-901585-2

First published in the United States, 2014
Library of Congress Control Number: 2014935385

Summary: Four friends work together to revive their school's
drama and music program.

RECYCLED
Paper made from recycled material
FSC® C103567
www.fsc.org

Orca Book Publishers is dedicated to preserving the environment and has printed this book on Forest Stewardship Council® certified paper.

Orca Book Publishers gratefully acknowledges the support for its publishing programs provided by the following agencies: the Government of Canada through the Canada Book Fund and the Canada Council for the Arts, and the Province of British Columbia through the BC Arts Council and the Book Publishing Tax Credit.

Cover design by Chantal Gabriell
Cover image by ESP Guitar Company, Dreamstime
Author photo by John Major

ORCA BOOK PUBLISHERS
PO Box 5626, Stn. B
Victoria, BC Canada
V8R 6S4

ORCA BOOK PUBLISHERS
PO Box 468
Custer, WA USA
98240-0468

www.orcabook.com
Printed and bound in Canada.

17 16 15 14 • 4 3 2 1

To my daughters, Zoey and Molly

ONE

Hit by a Thunderbolt

The electric guitar sat on a lopsided orange-and-gold sofa on the curb at the end of someone's driveway. Its glossy body gleamed in the wintry late-afternoon sun—a jet-black arrowhead blazing with two red thunderbolts. In the cold January light, its six silver tuning pegs winked like the crystals in the snow that covered the front lawn. Maybe it was a sign—a signal—to Wilmot Binkle as he trudged down the sidewalk on his way home from school.

Wilmot was walking home alone, as usual. He was dragging his feet, as usual, because he knew that when he opened the front door, there would be a long list of mathematical problems waiting for him to solve before his father got home from teaching at the university.

A kid should get a break between school and homework, Wilmot thought. He kicked a chunk of ice down the sidewalk. There should be a law or something.

At that moment, the guitar leaped into view, and the sight of it ripped through Wilmot's gloom like the opening chord of a rock-and-roll anthem.

An electric guitar.

What was it doing there, perched on the tattered upholstery of that ugly, three-legged sofa? Was it possible—could it even *be* possible—that someone had thrown the guitar into the trash? Though still half a block away, Wilmot was drawn to it by an inexorable force.

Creeping closer, Wilmot feared that at any moment the guitar might vanish, might turn out to be nothing more than a figment of his imagination. But no, it was real. As he approached it, Wilmot could see that the guitar had been played by someone until it was almost worn out. Five of its six strings were gone, and the black lacquer of its body was scratched and chipped.

I can replace the strings, Wilmot thought. *I can fix the scratches with a little bit of black paint. If only the guitar could be mine.*

Wriggling his right hand out of its woolen mitten, which stayed stuck in his jacket pocket, Wilmot reached out to touch the instrument. His fingers stroked the cold, shiny surface. He plucked the one remaining string.

"Hey, little dude!"

Wilmot jumped. He spun around, stumbled backward, fell over the arm of the sofa and landed on the frozen sidewalk, on top of his enormous backpack filled with heavy textbooks.

"I'm sorry, I didn't mean to, I'm really sorry!" Wilmot spluttered. Above him loomed a tall long-haired teenager.

The teenager reached down and yanked Wilmot to his feet.

"Chill," he said. "I didn't mean to scare you."

Despite the cold, Wilmot felt the palm of his hand breaking into a sweat. He yanked it out of the teenager's grip and stuffed it in his pocket. His eyes turned toward the guitar.

"Is it…is it yours?" he gasped out.

"That old guitar ain't mine to keep, little dude," said the teenager. "It was mine to play for a while. Y'know?"

Wilmot didn't know. But he didn't want to admit that he didn't know. He wasn't sure whether the teenager was mad at him. The guy didn't look mad, but it was hard to tell—he had metal piercings sticking out of his nose and eyebrows, and he was wearing a T-shirt with the word *Megadeth* on it. Wilmot didn't want to take any chances.

"I thought someone put it in the trash," he said.

"Not the trash, little dude. I put it out so someone would find it. A rebel vigilante. A midnight rambler. A jukebox hero. Now do you get it?"

Wilmot still didn't totally get it. But he grasped the part about someone else finding it. Someone else… maybe himself.

"Could I…could I have it?"

"Little dude!" said the teenager. "That's what I'm trying to tell you."

The teenager picked up the guitar and held it out to Wilmot. Wilmot's fingers curled around the cold fretboard. He cradled the body in the crook of his right arm. The guitar felt as though it belonged there—as though it had always belonged there.

He looked up at the pierced face of the teenager. Now that he wasn't so nervous, Wilmot thought he recognized him.

"Lester?"

"Shh!" The teenager glanced up and down the street.

Wilmot lowered his voice. "Weren't you my…baby-sitter? Like, when I was a little kid?"

"Yeah. That was before I got this"—he pointed to the spike in his eyebrow—"and this"—he touched the ring in his nose—"and this"—he stuck out his tongue and waggled the metal stud pierced through it. "And I changed my name to Headcase."

"Oh. Good name," said Wilmot. He was pretty sure his dad would disown him if *he* ever changed his name to Headcase. "And thanks for the guitar. But…why?"

"Come with me, little dude," said Headcase. "I'll show you."

He turned and loped down the driveway toward a tall red-brick house. Wilmot followed him, excited and nervous. He climbed the stairs of the rickety front porch, past a snow-dusted bicycle chained to the wooden railing, and watched as Headcase opened the front door, took a key out of his pocket and opened a second, inner door marked *Apartment 1-A*.

Headcase stepped inside. Grasping the guitar, Wilmot followed him.

The front hallway of Apartment 1-A smelled of stinky running shoes, old wallpaper and Kraft Dinner. To the right, a doorway opened into a large room with a fireplace in it, which looked like it was supposed to be a living room. The room was bare except for a mattress on the floor and a pile of dirty laundry, and some bedsheets hung over the windows instead of curtains. The teenager kicked aside a pile of junk mail from the hallway floor, opened a door to the left and led the way down a narrow flight of stairs to the basement.

Wilmot followed.

The basement smelled of even stinkier running shoes, mixed with greasy pizza boxes and grungy carpeting. But in an instant, Wilmot forgot about the odor. For in front of him stood the most amazing array of rock 'n' roll gear that he had ever set eyes on.

"Wow!" he breathed. "What is all this stuff?"

"Harmon Kardon receiver, authentic 1974 Pioneer turntable with diamond-tipped needle—my dad gave me that—six-CD changer, equalizer, reverberator, subwoofer, JBL speakers, Hackintosh computer—I built it from scratch from parts I got off the Internet—webcam and MIDI keyboard. And this"—Headcase turned to a wall lined with plastic milk crates, stacked sideways and crammed with hundreds of CDs and vinyl records—"is my awesome collection of Rock Through the Ages. Everything from Chuck Berry to Green Day and beyond. I got it all right here, little dude. But what you really came to see is this."

He flicked on a switch and a red spotlight illuminated a blood-red guitar gleaming on a silver guitar stand. Headcase stepped forward and flicked on the amplifier.

"Orange Thunderverb 200," he said. "Dual-function footswitch, multi-channel soundboard and this…" He picked up the guitar. "A Fender Vintage Hot Rod '57 Stratocaster. Won it in a radio contest. Sick."

Headcase slung the guitar strap over his shoulder. The instrument rode low across his hips. He stood for a moment, his head bowed as though in deep meditation. He raised his hand high in the air and brought it slashing down across the strings. A chord stabbed through the silence of the room, and Wilmot felt it pierce his heart.

Headcase launched into a wailing guitar solo. His left hand spidered up and down the fretboard; his right hand jittered over the strings. The notes grew louder, faster, more frantic, until they blurred into one another. The solo rose to a crescendo of distorted chords, a sound like the screech of a hundred-car freight train jamming on the brakes in a lonely stretch of prairieland, a final echoing crash, and then…

Silence.

"Wooooo-hoooo!" howled Headcase.

"Wooooo-hoooo!" howled Wilmot.

"Waaaaaaaaaaaaaaaaaah!" screamed Headcase.

"Waaaaaaaaaaaaaaaaaah!" screamed Wilmot.

"Bang your head!" shouted Headcase.

Wilmot banged his head.

"Rock on!" yelled Headcase. He pumped his fist in the air, index and pinkie fingers outstretched in the universal symbol of rock 'n' roll.

"Rock on!" yelled Wilmot, pumping the rock-and-roll symbol with his own fist.

Headcase fell backward into a threadbare orange-and-gold armchair. There was no other furniture in the room, so Wilmot fell to the floor.

"Your turn, little dude." Headcase held out the guitar to him.

Wilmot blushed and stuttered, "No, I…I don't really know how to play yet."

"Cool. I'll catch it later then," said Headcase. He jumped out of his chair. "Hey, look, I'll help you out, little dude."

Before Wilmot realized what was happening, Headcase had pulled a cardboard box out of a corner and rummaged around in it until he found five new guitar strings. He strung them on the old guitar and tuned it up.

"Wow, thanks," said Wilmot.

Headcase handed him the guitar.

"Live without warning, little dude."

"Okay," said Wilmot.

"And call me if you have any trouble getting things set up."

He scrawled a phone number on a scrap of paper and shoved it into Wilmot's hand as they walked up the stairs toward the front door.

Outside, the cold wind nipped Wilmot's fingers, but he left his woolen mittens stuffed in his jacket pockets. It felt safer to carry the guitar in his bare hands than risk it slipping out of his grasp. The extra weight of the instrument should have made him feel heavier. But instead, he felt lighter, like a kid in zero gravity.

He had a guitar, his very own guitar.

Now, if only he could sneak it past his father.

TWO

Smuggling the Six-String

The sun hovered low in the sky as Wilmot turned the corner and headed down the block toward his house. He should have been home at least an hour ago. His dad was going to chew him out.

Wilmot's boots crunched on the snow as he cut across his neighbor's lawn, ducked through the hedge and came out in his own backyard, between the laundry line and the aluminum garden shed. He couldn't go in through the front door, where his father would surely be waiting for him. His dad hated rock music. In fact, he liked silence better than any music at all. He was always busy reading or working, and he wouldn't let Wilmot turn on the radio in the house or get an MP3 player. Not a chance that he'd let him keep the electric guitar, if he ever found out about it. But the back door opened into the laundry room, and this was a key element in the plan that Wilmot had concocted during his walk home from Headcase's apartment.

He turned the key. The back door swung open. Warm air, perfumed with the lavender smell of fabric softener, billowed around him. He closed the door and wriggled his feet out of their boots. No one called a greeting. So far, so good.

Wilmot shrugged off his backpack and quietly set it on the floor, beside the basket of clean laundry his mother had been reminding him to take upstairs since the weekend. Lucky thing he'd forgotten. He burrowed a hole in the laundry, nestled his guitar inside and covered it with a camouflage of T-shirts and underwear.

The neck of the guitar stuck out.

Drat. A glitch in his plan.

Carefully, he pushed the guitar neck down into the basket. The body of the guitar popped out the other end.

Drat.

The black paint of the guitar body winked at Wilmot like the eye of an outlaw. The red lightning bolts whispered to him: "Rock on."

Wilmot smothered the lightning bolts in a heap of unmatched socks.

The neck popped out the other end again.

Drat and double-drat.

The guitar's steel strings shone. The silver tuning keys gleamed. The neck of the guitar rose proudly from the laundry basket, like a Waving Flag of Rock 'n' Roll Freedom.

Wilmot shoved a purple sock over it.

Now it looked like a Suspicious Something Hidden in the Laundry Basket with a Purple Sock on Top.

What am I going to do? thought Wilmot.

Footsteps sounded in the hallway.

Wilmot ripped the sock off the guitar. A string twanged. He smothered it with a pair of SpongeBob underpants. The footsteps came closer. Wilmot looked around frantically. There, inside the dryer! A fluffy duvet pressed up against the clear glass door. Wilmot lunged for the dryer, grabbed the billowy bedspread and stuffed it on top of the laundry basket, smothering all trace of the guitar.

The door opened. His father peered down at him.

"Wilmot! It's five thirty!"

His father's black eyebrows rose in peaks above his eyes. His black beard arrowed down in a V beneath his chin. Everything about his father was sharp, and for a moment Wilmot feared that his sharp eyes would pierce right through the duvet and spy the guitar underneath.

"Sorry, Dad. I was just hanging out with some guys from the chess club."

Wilmot hated lying to his dad, but how could he tell him that he'd spent the past hour screaming and banging his head in the basement apartment of a teenage kid with spikes pierced through his face? Obviously, he couldn't.

"I don't know how you expect to get your math worksheet done. And your homework. I've told you a hundred times, Wilmot: you won't excel if you don't apply yourself."

"I'll start right after supper, Dad." Wilmot took cover behind the fluffy duvet. His palms broke into a sweat. This always happened when his dad got angry at him. If it continued, his forehead would start to sweat, and it would drip into his eyes, and—

"Taking the laundry up, Wilmot? That's very helpful." His mom appeared in the doorway. Where Wilmot's dad was all sharp and pointy, his mother was the opposite—all round and soft. Where his dad liked to create arguments, his mother liked to avoid them.

She was always trying to smooth things over and make everyone happy.

"That laundry basket's been sitting there for three days," said his father.

"You see? And now he's taking it up," Mom said. "Go ahead, dear. Up you go."

"I'll fold and sort it too, Mom," Wilmot promised, scrambling up the stairs to the safety of his bedroom.

He fell to his knees in relief as he closed the door behind him. He tore the duvet off the laundry basket and flung it on his bed. There it was. The guitar. His guitar.

He lifted it gently and curled the fingers of his left hand around the fretboard. The metal strings pressed painfully into his tender fingertips. Wilmot didn't care. Real guitar players didn't feel pain. Real guitar players had calluses where their nerve endings should be. He stroked the fingers of his right hand over the strings. The sound rang out, faint but true. If only he could plug the guitar into an amp and crank up the volume. If only he could let out a scream like he had in the teenager's basement—waaaaaaaaaaaaaaaaaah!

Get a grip, he told himself. A scream like that would blow his cover.

Wilmot laid the guitar on his bed and turned to the task of folding the laundry as he'd promised his mom.

Maybe she would understand about the guitar. Maybe she'd even help him, if he told her his secret. But Wilmot couldn't risk it. Because when it came to arguments over really important things, his mom never stood up to his dad. His dad always won in the end. No, he had to keep the guitar a secret from his parents. And he had to get it out of the house before they discovered it.

Luckily, he had help that he could count on: the help of Dunces Anonymous.

Dunces Anonymous was the club started by his new friend, Josh Johnson. A club "for kids who aren't as good at stuff as their parents think they should be," Josh called it. That described Wilmot perfectly. Over the Christmas holidays, Wilmot had persuaded his father to let him transfer to Josh's school by telling him about the school's amazing enriched math program. Wilmot figured he could survive enriched math, but of course that wasn't the real reason he wanted to transfer to Oakview Public School. The first real reason was Dunces Anonymous. The second real reason was the school's Drama and Music program.

Drama and Music was an optional course that kids in grades five to eight could take twice a week instead of Visual Arts. The school didn't have enough instruments to go around, so you could only join the course by lottery—or if you had your own instrument. If Wilmot could smuggle his guitar to school, he could join the Drama and Music program and learn to play. It wasn't too late. They were less than a week into the winter semester. Best of all, his father never needed to know a thing about it.

Wilmot looked down at the heap of laundry in the basket and the small pile of folded T-shirts beside it. What was the point of folding clothes, anyway? They just got all rumpled again when you wore them. Might as well just stuff them in the drawers, he figured. With the laundry done, he crept to the bed and picked up the guitar. It throbbed and pulsed in his hands. He needed a safe hiding place for it until he took it to school.

Wilmot looked around his room. The closet? No. Someone might find it if they came looking for extra bedsheets. Under the bed? Yes. Lying on his belly, he reached for the long, flat cardboard box where his mother stowed his extra wool sweaters. Wilmot buried the guitar under the bottom layer of sweaters, closed the box and shoved it into the deepest, darkest corner.

"Rock on," he whispered.

"Rock on," the guitar, muffled by wooly sweaters, seemed to whisper back to him.

He opened his bedroom door a crack and peered into the hallway. No one there. He could hear his parents' voices downstairs. Daringly, Wilmot slipped into his father's study, grabbed the cordless phone from its cradle and scuttled back to his room.

He dialed Josh's number.

"Josh, you're not going to believe this," Wilmot whispered. "I've got a guitar! I'm joining Drama and Music!"

There was silence on the other end of the line for a moment.

"Wilmot, haven't you heard?" Josh said finally. "The principal just canceled the Drama and Music program."

THREE

Operation Rescue Drama and Music

Hunched in the leather armchair in Josh's living room, Wilmot stared at the marshmallows floating in his mug of hot cocoa. Normally, he loved marshmallows, all plump and soft and soaked with chocolaty sweetness. But today they looked like the knuckles of a dead man's hand floating in muddy swamp water. He felt as though evil forces were conspiring against him.

It was Friday after school, and Josh had called an emergency meeting of Dunces Anonymous at his place, a condo on the sixth floor of a swanky, modern building. Wilmot knew he'd be home late from school.

He knew he'd have to lie to his dad about the reason why. He didn't care.

Wilmot Binkle was a desperate kid.

"Don't worry, Wil." Josh put a hand on his shoulder. "It's going to be okay."

"If I can't learn to play that guitar, Josh, my life is over."

"I told you, don't worry. The Dunces are on the case."

Wilmot poked at a marshmallow while Josh handed mugs of hot chocolate to Wang and Magnolia, the two other members of the club. He wanted to believe that Dunces Anonymous had the power to bring back the Drama and Music program. But what could four kids do against the mighty power of adults?

"Okay," said Josh. "Let's get started. Wilmot needs us to come up with a cunning plan to save the Drama and Music program."

"It's not just Wilmot. What about me?" interrupted Magnolia. "I can't believe they're canceling drama! Just when I was preparing to audition for the lead role in *Nocturnia, Vampire Princess of Doom*!"

Magnolia jumped onto a leather footstool and drew in a breath. Despite his deep gloom, Wilmot couldn't help staring at her. She was draped from head to toe in a purple gothic gown festooned with fake cobwebs.

Her fingernails were an inch long and blood red. Around her neck hung a necklace of tiny human skulls. She was obviously trying to grow her hair long, but instead of being black and silky—which was how Wilmot pictured a vampire's hair—Magnolia's was brown, frizzy and sticking out wildly all over her head. Sleeping in a coffin—which vampires were supposed to do—had apparently given Nocturnia a bad case of bed head. Wilmot didn't say that to Magnolia though. She might be offended.

Magnolia lifted her arms to command silence. "Nocturnia, Vampire Princess of Doom, rises from the grave to avenge the death of her brother Vladimir at the hands of their archenemy, the indomitable Prince Benedictus of Transylvania!"

"Cool!" said Wang.

"Yeah, cool." Magnolia flopped down on the footstool. "And now it's canceled, thanks to Principal Hale and his dumb hockey team."

"Is that why?" Wilmot asked. *Hockey? A bunch of jocks chasing a puck around a rink? Was that the reason the principal had quashed his rock 'n' roll dreams?*

"That's what my mom said. She went to the Parent Council meeting this week," said Magnolia. "You know Monsieur Guillaume, the French teacher? Well,

I guess his wife had a heart attack over Christmas and he decided to retire. So, instead of hiring a new French teacher, the principal told Mrs. Karloff that she has to teach French this semester. Which means she can't teach Drama and Music anymore. And since the school is saving soooo much money by not hiring a new French teacher, the principal decided to spend the money on a hockey team."

"Is he allowed to do that?" said Josh.

"My mom said the Parent Council all got behind him. She said he gave this big speech about how hockey was the 'beating heart of our culture.'"

Magnolia struck her heart for emphasis.

"Sheesh! What about real culture? What about drama? What about music?"

"Yeah, what about Nickelback?" said Wilmot.

"What about Justin Bieber?" said Josh.

"Justin Bieber? Give me a break!" Magnolia groaned.

"Okay, forget the Biebs," said Josh. "But seriously, what's so great about hockey?"

"Ask Stacey Hogarth's mom," said Magnolia. "She's the head of the Parent Council."

"Stacey's mom? What does she care about hockey?"

"I guess Stacey plays." Magnolia shrugged.

"Great, so now it's us against Stacey," said Josh. "Again!"

"We must fight her to the death!" Wang jumped from his armchair, plucked a long reed from a dried-flower arrangement in the corner and executed a sequence of fancy sword-fighting moves. Wilmot looked on dispiritedly. He didn't see how sword fighting would help them—unless Wang challenged the principal to a duel—which might be a good idea, but it seemed unlikely to happen.

"Wait! I know!" Magnolia spread her arms and arose from the footstool. "Nocturnia, Vampire Princess of Doom, ascends from her grave to avenge the cancellation of the Drama and Music program! Suddenly, strange things begin happening at Oakview Public School. Weird puncture marks appear on the necks of innocent kids. Students wander through the hallways, dazed…"

"Students already wander through the hallways, dazed," Josh pointed out.

"A cryptic message, written in blood, appears mysteriously on the principal's door," Magnolia continued. "*Bring back the Drama and Music program, or dire doom will befall the school. Heed this warning! Before it is Too Late!*"

Silence hung in the room following Magnolia's performance. Finally, Josh said, "I don't think he's going to fall for that."

"Why not?" said Magnolia.

"Everyone knows that vampires aren't real."

"Well, sheesh! If we have to stick to stuff that's real…"

Magnolia flopped back down on the footstool.

Josh cast Wilmot a reassuring look. "Remember what they say in chess club: know the mind of your opponent."

Easy for you to say, Wilmot thought. Josh was good at chess. In chess, knowing your opponent's mind was supposed to help you figure out his moves and, therefore, defeat him. Wilmot could never figure out his opponent's moves. Half the time, he couldn't even figure out his own moves. No wonder he was so lousy at chess.

"So, what do we know about Principal Hale?" Josh continued.

"He likes hockey," Wang offered.

"Well, duh," said Magnolia.

"What else?" said Josh.

No one said anything. Wilmot's mind felt as blank and squishy as one of the marshmallows in his hot chocolate. What did he know about the principal? Exactly nothing. This was hopeless.

"I know!" Wang cried out at last, brandishing the dried reed. "We must reconnoiter enemy territory! Penetrate his inner sanctum! Probe the depths of his hidden lair! Uncover his darkest secrets!"

"What are you talking about?" said Magnolia.

"I mean, we have to go snoop around his office and find out some stuff about him. Then we can figure out how to change his mind about canceling Drama and Music."

"Good thinking," said Josh. "How do we sneak into the principal's office?"

"You don't sneak into a principal's office, dodo," said Magnolia. "You get sent there. Like, for doing bad stuff."

"Bad stuff?" Wilmot looked at her in alarm. "We can't do bad stuff!"

"We're Dunces Anonymous, Wilmot!" Wang stabbed an imaginary enemy with his reed. "Bad Stuff is our middle name!"

"It's not, actually," Josh clarified. "And we don't do really bad stuff. Just stuff that's a little bit...against the rules."

"And only when adults are being completely unreasonable." Magnolia rolled her eyes.

"But Josh…" Wilmot felt himself beginning to sweat. "I can't do bad stuff. I really can't. I'll get in so much trouble. My dad…you don't understand—"

"It's okay, Wil," Josh interrupted. "You don't have to do the bad stuff. I'll do it."

"You…you will?"

"Yeah," said Josh.

Wilmot looked at Josh in disbelief. Never before had anyone offered to take on his troubles for him. Wilmot began to feel a tiny bit of hope rise to the surface of his heart. Like a marshmallow bobbing in a cup of hot chocolate.

"He's the prez!" Wang slapped Josh on the back. "Getting in trouble for other people is his job."

"I guess you could say that." Josh sighed. "So, how am I going to get sent to the principal's office?"

"You could pull the fire alarm," Wang suggested.

"Thanks, Wang," said Josh sarcastically. "I want to get sent to the office, not expelled from school."

"It has to be something just a little bit bad," Wilmot reminded them, already feeling guilty about getting Josh into trouble.

"Think!" Wang waved the reed over his head, pacing the room. "Think, think, think!"

"I know!" Magnolia broke in. "You could pull my hair in class."

"You think that'd work?" Josh said.

"Try it." Magnolia turned her head and shook her frizzy mop at him. Josh grabbed a clump of it and tugged. Magnolia fell to the carpet with a bloodcurdling scream.

"Ow! My hair! My hair!" Magnolia shrieked, writhing on the ground. "Josh pulled my hair!"

Wilmot jumped from his armchair.

"Magnolia, are you okay? Josh, she's really hurt…"

This was all wrong. He didn't mean for his friends to hurt each other. He didn't mean…

Magnolia jumped to her feet, grinned and took a bow.

"That was great," said Josh.

"Works for me," said Wang.

"You mean, you weren't really hurt?" said Wilmot.

"I was acting, Wilmot! Sheesh! If you thought that was good, wait till you see me in *Nocturnia, Vampire Princess of Doom!*"

Magnolia struck a vampire pose. Josh slung his arm around Wilmot's shoulders.

"Monday morning, the Dunces swing into action!" he announced. "Code name: Operation Rescue Drama and Music."

FOUR

The Path of Enlightenment

Wang leaped into the air with a flying kick and landed in a fighting stance, facing the mirror. He ducked, spun, parried an invisible opponent, crouched low and threw a perfect back handspring. He was the man with the moves. The boy with the grooves. The kid with the skid, the guy with the fly, the warrior with the—what rhymed with warrior? Oh well, it didn't matter. He was ready to take on all challengers for the glory of dancing the lion dance.

It was quarter to eight on Saturday morning, fifteen minutes before class was supposed to start, but already the fitness room of the community center was packed. There must have been thirty or forty kids, although the mirrors that lined the walls made it look like hundreds more. A jabber of Chinese and English filled the air. Some of the kids were practicing Kung Fu moves. Others were stretching or sitting around and talking. One kid was spinning upside down on one shoulder, her legs whirling in the air like helicopter blades. That would be Zahraa, a girl from school who took break-dancing classes too.

Wang knew a bunch of other kids in the class too: Shawn and Al Tung, Fengzhen Liu and lots of others with Chinese parents or grandparents, and some kids who weren't Chinese at all, including Josh, who wasn't even good at dancing and had only signed up because Wang talked him into it.

Josh hurried into class at five minutes to eight and flung himself on the floor next to Wang.

"Whew! I thought I wasn't going to make it."

"What happened to you?"

"I missed my first bus and I had to run for the second."

"Couldn't your mom drive you?"

"She said I wanted to sign up for this, so it was my responsibility to get here." He shrugged. "I showed her that pamphlet. You know, the one you gave me? She said Larry sounds like a fake."

Wang shook his head.

"She just doesn't understand. Parents don't like it when other people are smarter than them."

Wang thought it was disrespectful to call their teacher Larry. That had been his name once, long ago. But after a three-year pilgrimage to the mystical monasteries of China, he had returned home with the new, Chinese name Hui Bing, meaning "wise warrior." His brain held the wisdom of a thousand Chinese scholars. At least, that's what the pamphlet said.

On his return home, Hui Bing (formerly Larry) had brought with him a traditional Chinese lion costume. The lion's head was made of sculpted rice paper on a bent bamboo frame. It was painted in fiery red and yellow, with a jewel-encrusted horn. It had great, glittering eyes, pom-pommed ears that moved back and forth and a huge mouth that opened and closed with the pull of a string.

Hui Bing had learned the lion dance from his Kung Fu master in China, and to share his knowledge, he had offered to teach a class to kids at the community center. At the end of the ten-week class, the two best students would perform the traditional lion dance in full costume at the community center's talent show.

Wang was determined to be chosen.

"I heard Hui Bing is so smart, *nobody* can understand him," Wang said. "In fact, I heard he's so smart, even his *own brain* can't understand him."

"How is that possible?" said Josh.

Before Wang could explain, the hands on the clock hit 8, and Master Hui Bing himself strode through the door.

He was tall and muscular. His massive hands, powerful enough to karate-chop through a stack of solid bricks, swung by his sides. He wore a crisp white Kung Fu uniform, tied at the waist with a black belt, the sign of high mastery of the martial arts. His blond, wavy hair flowed down his back like a lion's mane. Reaching the center of the room, he pivoted, stopped and fixed the class with a penetrating gaze. As though by magic, the kids fell silent and arranged themselves into rows.

The master bowed. The rows of kids bowed back.

"You have come to learn the lion dance," Hui Bing said in a deep, powerful voice. "Understand this: You do not choose the lion. The lion chooses you. You do not dance the lion. The lion dances you. To dance the lion, you must know the wisdom of the lion. Now, we begin."

The wisdom of the lion? Wang's stomach clenched. Learning the dance steps was one thing. But wisdom?

Wisdom was not exactly Wang's strong point. He snuck a glance around the room. He knew at least a dozen kids who got better marks in school than he did. How could he compete? How could he learn the wisdom of the lion? *Focus*, Wang told himself. *Focus on the master.*

"Horse stance!" Master Hui Bing barked. "Feet apart! Knees bent! Arms up!"

Wang and the other kids jumped into horse stance. The master paced back and forth in front of them. "Shawn! Knees bent! Fengzhen! Straight back! Wang! Strong arms!" he called. "The stream springs from the heart of the mountain, but who knows the heart of the lonely rutabaga?"

A piece of wisdom! Wang thought. *I must hold it in my brain! But what does it mean? Who knows the heart of the lonely rutabaga?*

"Hey, Wang," Josh whispered. "What's a rutabaga?"

Wang turned his head slightly, not budging from horse stance.

"It's like a turnip," he whispered back.

Josh scrunched up his face.

"Who knows the heart of the lonely *turnip*?"

That sounded weird, Wang had to admit. But Master Hui Bing hadn't said "turnip," he had said "rutabaga." There must be something special about a rutabaga, something profound and inscrutable. The syllables, maybe, had a mystic meaning: Ru-Ta-Ba-Ga...

Master Hui Bing tossed his hair and clapped his hands. The kids sprang out of horse stance.

"Good. Now we learn the unicorn step. One leg crossed over the other, moving sideways. Three steps to the left, and change direction. Three steps to the right, and change direction."

The master demonstrated, clapping and calling out the steps as he pranced in front of them with the grace of a unicorn. "Cross, cross, cross, change direction. Cross, cross, cross, change direction! Now you!"

Clap, clap, clap! The master's hands struck the beat as the kids began to move in unicorn step. But this was trickier than standing still in horse stance. Some of the kids stepped right. Some of the kids stepped left. Some of the kids jumped back into horse stance. A kid named Derek stood there picking his nose.

The kids who'd stepped right slammed into the kids who'd stepped left. The kids who'd stepped left stumbled into the horse-stance kids. The horse-stance kids shoved them off and they went stumbling around the room, bumping into other kids, knocking each other down. The nose-picker suddenly realized he was supposed to be doing something. He tripped over his own feet, turned a half-pirouette and face-planted on the floor. All over the room, bodies were flying.

But Wang, trained to avoid his fallen opponents in his sword-fighting classes, unicorn-stepped nimbly around his classmates. *Cross, cross, cross, change direction. Cross, cross, cross, change direction.* Maybe he had a chance of being chosen to dance the lion after all!

Clapping time, Master Hui Bing spoke again. "The flower of youth may bloom in a bathtub," he proclaimed, "but where shall the wise man wash his socks?"

Another piece of wisdom! Wang seized on it and repeated it to himself as he unicorn-stepped around the fallen bodies: The flower (*cross*) of youth (*cross*) may bloom (*cross*) in a bathtub (*change direction*). But where (*cross*) shall the wise (*cross*) man wash (*cross*) his socks (*change direction*)?

"Psst. Hey, Wang!" Josh fell in beside him. "How'd the wise man get his socks dirty?"

"His socks?" How *did* the wise man get his socks dirty? If he was so wise, couldn't he keep his socks clean? Wang's mother would certainly think so. Changing direction on cue, Wang looked toward the master—his flowing hair, his powerful hands, his clear blue eyes. A bolt of pure wisdom shot from those eyes straight into Wang's mind. He knew the answer.

He turned toward Josh.

"On the path of enlightenment," he whispered.

"Huh?" Josh missed a step and fumbled to catch up. But Wang felt electrified by his newfound insight. He pondered it as he continued to unicorn-step in time: The path (*cross*) of enlightenment (*cross*) is long (*cross*) and muddy (*change direction*). But where (*cross*) shall the wise (*cross*) man wash (*cross*) his socks (*cross*)?

In that split second, Wang realized that he'd crossed when he should have changed direction. It was too late now. Josh—who for once had changed direction at the proper time—rammed into him from the left. Wang stumbled right. Another kid bumped into him from the right. He stumbled left. Josh bumped into him again. He stumbled backward. He stepped on the body of a kid lying on the floor. He felt himself losing balance and flung out a hand, grasping at anything to stop from falling, but his hand closed around Josh's arm, and instead of steadying him, Josh crashed down on top of him. Another kid tripped and fell on top of them, and another, and before he could pull an escape maneuver, Wang found himself squashed at the bottom of a pile of groaning, squirming kids.

Meanwhile, oblivious to his plight, the master's hands continued to clap the time.

The wise man walks the path of enlightenment, Wang thought, *but why am I smothered in stinky armpits?*

FIVE

To Be or Not To Be

At eleven o'clock Monday morning, the classroom door swished open and in waltzed Madame Karloff, formerly Mrs. Karloff, the Drama and Music teacher, and now the *professeure de Français*.

Josh leaned forward and poked Magnolia in the back.

"Does she even speak French?"

Magnolia shrugged. "Who cares? She's got a great costume."

It was true. The principal might have canceled the Drama and Music program, but he couldn't cancel the drama in Madame Karloff. She was wearing a red beret, a red silk scarf and red high-heeled shoes, each heel shaped like an upside-down miniature Eiffel Tower. Her short dress was striped red, white and blue like the French flag. She breezed across the room, blowing kisses and exclaiming, "*Bonjour, mes chéries! Bonjour!*"

Josh glanced away from the French teacher and back at Magnolia's fuzzy ponytail, which dangled in front of him like the emergency brake on a subway train. Once he pulled it, the class would come screeching to a stop—and knowing Magnolia, *screeching* was exactly the right word. Somehow, he was finding it hard to get up his nerve.

It wasn't that he intended to wimp out of their plan. It was just that so far, it never seemed to be the right time to cause a kerfuffle. Not during the national anthem or the moment of silent reflection. Not during the surprise spelling quiz that Mr. Bogg had sprung on them and not during math, which was Josh's favorite subject and which he didn't want to ruin by being sent to the office. Still, when he looked back at the last row and saw the despondent look on Wilmot's face, he knew his friend was losing faith in him. Catching Wilmot's eye, he gave him a covert thumbs-up and turned back to the front of the class just as Madame Karloff raised her hands for silence.

"*Mes chéries*," she began. "French is not merely a language. It is a *petit peu* of a *quelque chose. Mon Dieu!* It is a *soupçon* of a *je ne sais quoi!* It is a *raison d'être!* It is a *mode de vie!* It is a *quiche au fromage!* In short, it is a feeling! Now, I'd like you all to take a moment, close your eyes and *feel* French."

Josh closed his eyes and tried to concentrate. What did French feel like? A baguette? He didn't feel like a baguette. It was too skinny. Too crusty. A croissant? Did he feel like a croissant? No, it was too curvy. Too buttery. A poodle? Maybe he felt like a poodle. *Wouf.* Josh barked experimentally under his breath. *Wouf. Wouf.* Josh didn't feel like a poodle. He didn't feel French at all. He felt like an idiot.

Madame Karloff heaved a deep sigh, signaling that it was time for the students to open their eyes.

"Now that you are all in character, we may begin. Today, we shall study the verb *être*—'to be.'"

She turned and wrote on the blackboard: *être—to be.*

Conjugating verbs! Josh thought gratefully. The boringest thing in the universe. If there was ever a good time to yank Magnolia's hair, verb conjugation had to be it. But when Madame Karloff turned back toward the class, a strange light gleamed in her eyes.

"Darlings!" She glanced around conspiratorially. "I know this isn't drama class, but tell me, have any of you studied Shakespeare?"

A few hands went up.

"Then perhaps you know the great speech from Hamlet!" she exclaimed. "*Être, ou ne pas être! To be, or not to be!*"

Magnolia turned around and looked at Josh. Her eyes, too, were gleaming. Josh had a funny feeling that French class was about to go seriously off the rails.

Madame Karloff clutched her hand to her heart.

"*Être, ou ne pas être! To be, or not to be: that is the question!*" she exclaimed. "You see, darlings, Hamlet is asking himself whether he should live or whether he should die! He is seething with anguish! Desperately, he clutches to the last threads that bind him to this mortal world! To be, or not to be? To live, or not to live? *Être, ou ne pas être?* Would anyone in the class like to give us a dramatic recital?"

Magnolia's hand shot up.

"Yes, Magnolia, go ahead, *darling!*"

Magnolia stood up beside her desk.

"*To be, or not to be,*" she began, lifting a hand to her brow, "*that is the question!*"

Looking at the back of Magnolia's frizzy head, Josh decided he'd better pull her hair soon, before French class got any weirder. He would never get a better opportunity. The class had fallen silent and Madame Karloff was listening with rapt attention as Magnolia moaned on about "the slings and arrows of outrageous fortune." Now was the right dramatic moment—as Magnolia herself might say—to cause a disruption.

Josh reached up and yanked Magnolia's hair.

Magnolia ignored him.

"*To die! To sleep! To sleep: perchance to dream!*" she exclaimed. "*For in that sleep of death what dreams may come, when we have shuffled off this mortal coil!*"

What on earth was a mortal coil? Josh wondered. How did you shuffle one? Like a deck of cards? Why was this Shakespeare guy so famous if the stuff he wrote didn't make any sense? What did it matter anyway? The thing that mattered was helping Wilmot. Magnolia definitely wasn't helping.

Josh reached out and yanked her hair harder. Magnolia's shoulders gave a little shrug.

"*For who would bear the whips and scorns of time,*" she sighed.

Josh reached out a third time and yanked as hard as he could.

"*The oppressor's wrong*," Magnolia continued, thumping her chest, "*the proud man's contumely, the pangs of dispriz'd l-o-o-o-o-o-ve...*"

It was hopeless. Trying to stop Magnolia in the middle of a dramatic monologue was like trying to stop a parent in the middle of a lecture about cleaning your room. Josh even knew what she'd say about it when he confronted her later on. She'd say she was an Actress, and she had a duty to her Art. The Show Must Go On, she'd say. Well, Josh was the president of Dunces Anonymous and he had a duty to Wilmot—Wilmot, sitting in the back row with his arms crossed on his desk, his head slumped between them, while Magnolia blithely continued her speech. "*Who'd these fardels bear*," she cried, "*to grunt and sweat under a weary life?*"

Wilmot looked like a kid who was grunting and sweating under a weary life, Josh thought. He probably had lots of fardels to bear too—whatever fardels were. They must be pretty bad, the way Magnolia was groaning on about them.

He must make one last attempt to help his friend! Searching his mind desperately for a plan B, Josh caught sight of a second head of hair—a sleek, chestnut-colored ponytail that looked nothing like Magnolia's messy frizz. The ponytail was perfectly brushed and fastened with a black hair elastic. It hung down neatly between the shoulder blades of a girl in the row next to him. It was so close that Josh could pull it simply by reaching out his hand.

The ponytail belonged to Stacey Hogarth.

Josh felt his fingers tingle.

He shouldn't pull Stacey's ponytail. He knew he shouldn't. It was against school rules. And besides, it wasn't nice. But Josh couldn't help thinking of all the mean things Stacey had done to him. How she'd tried to take over Dunces Anonymous and kick him out of the club. How she'd tattled on him to the principal about setting off the school fire alarm. How her mom had been in cahoots with the principal to cancel the Drama and Music program so that Stacey could play on the hockey team.

I'll just give it a little tug, he thought. *It won't really hurt.*

His fingers caught hold of the silky strands.

"Thus conscience does make cowards of us all!" Magnolia exclaimed.

Josh tugged.

"Owwwwweeeeeeee!" screamed Stacey.

"And thus the native hue of resolution…" Magnolia fumbled to a stop.

Silence fell in the classroom. Madame Karloff turned her fiery eyes on Stacey.

"Stacey, *darling*, what is the meaning of this?"

"It's Josh Johnson!" Stacey howled. She jumped from her seat and pointed her finger at him. "He pulled my ponytail, *Madame*!"

The burning eyes of the teacher turned on Josh.

"Josh, is this true?"

Josh hung his head.

"*Oui, Madame.*"

Madame Karloff stamped her foot. The Eiffel Tower rapped the tile floor.

"What has gotten into you, Josh?" she demanded. "Really! Interrupting Shakespeare? The greatest playwright who ever lived?"

"And he pulled my hair!" Stacey butted in.

"Oh, yes, and you pulled that girl's hair." Madame Karloff waved dismissively at Stacey. "In any case, I am sending you to the principal's office immediately. I shall call down to explain the situation. And I hope you will have learned your lesson in the future."

Josh rose from his desk and slunk out of the classroom under the gloating eyes of Stacey Hogarth. But just before he slipped out the door, he turned to look at Wilmot. There, in the back corner of the room, Wilmot's face beamed at him with gratitude, as though a heavy fardel had been lifted from his weary shoulders.

SIX

Sweating Under the Fardels

Although pulling Stacey's ponytail might have seemed like a flash of brilliant inspiration at the time, it didn't seem like such a good idea now, as Josh sat on the hard wooden chair, waiting to be called into the principal's office.

What if he got into real trouble? What if the principal phoned his mom? She already had her doubts about Dunces Anonymous, especially after that time he got suspended for setting off the school fire alarm. Which wasn't really his fault, but still…what if his mom made him disband the club?

Remember your mission, Josh told himself. *Find out everything possible about Principal Hale. Know your opponent. Know his weaknesses. Remember, Operation Rescue Drama and Music is on your shoulders.*

From behind the closed door of the principal's office came the voice of a radio DJ: "And now, here's the latest from George Thorobred on Today's Best Country Hits, 101.5 The Twang!"

Principal likes country music, Josh noted.

A guitar strummed through the airwaves, accompanied by the nasal voice of George Thorobred.

*Oh, there's a tear in my beer
And a pain in my rear,
'Cause I've been ridin' all night
And darlin' you ain't here.
Now my tender heart is breakin'
Please tell me I'm mistaken
Please tell me you still love me,
'Cause my butt is really achin'…*

Correction, Josh thought. *Principal likes lame country music.*

The door swung open as George Thorobred launched into a banjo solo.

"Come in, Josh," the principal said sternly.

Principal Hale had a head like a squash: round and bald on the top, plump and jowly around the bottom. He was a big, heavy man and he wore a dark blue suit and tie, which made him look even bigger and heavier. Josh took a deep breath and told himself to remember his mission as he slid onto the chair in front of the principal's massive oak desk.

The principal walked around to the other side of his desk, flicked off the radio and sat down. Josh scanned the room for clues about the mind of the principal. A few family photos sat on the desk, showing some kids and a dog. On the walls hung framed pictures of the women's and men's Olympic hockey teams. There was also a framed picture of a mountain scene with bold letters that said:

A Principal's Vow
As principal, I vow to respect my school's staff, parents and, most of all, its students. I know that by helping young minds to grow, I, too, can achieve spiritual growth.

Josh wondered if Principal Hale really believed that or if he had just memorized it to pass the Principal Test at Principal School. If he really believed in respecting his students, why had he canceled the Drama and Music program? Josh wished he was brave enough to ask Principal Hale that question directly. But when he looked across the desk and saw the glare in the principal's eyes, the wrinkles on his forehead, his down-turned mouth, Josh decided to sit still and say nothing.

"Well, Josh," said the principal in a stern voice. "It seems you pulled Stacey Hogarth's hair in class. What do you have to say for yourself?"

"I didn't mean to, sir," Josh squeaked. "It was an accident. I'm really sorry."

"An accident. Hmph! Your teacher says that this incident occurred during a dramatic recital of Hamlet's 'To be, or not to be' speech."

"Yes, sir," Josh stammered. "I sort of got carried away."

"Carried away," the principal repeated flatly.

"Yes, sir." Josh felt a glimmer of inspiration, recalling the words of Madame Karloff. "You know, by *his seething anguish*."

"Seething anguish," the principal repeated in the same stern, flat voice.

"Yes, sir. Hamlet's. You know? His seething anguish?"

"Hmph," growled the principal. "And so, carried away by seething anguish, you grabbed this girl's ponytail?"

"I'd say it was more of a clutch than a grab, sir," Josh explained.

"A clutch."

"Yes, sir." Josh wished he had Magnolia's talent for acting. "You know, like Hamlet? Clutching on to the last threads that bound him to this mortal world?"

"Hmph." The principal's jowls quivered. "You're telling me that, carried away by Hamlet's seething anguish, you clutched Stacey Hogarth's ponytail as though it was the last thread binding you to this mortal world?"

"Um, yes, sir," said Josh. "It was the fardels," he added.

"The fardels."

"Yes, sir," said Josh. "He was grunting and sweating under the fardels. You know?"

"Who was?"

"Hamlet, sir."

"Under the fardels?"

"Yes, sir."

"What the heck is a fardel?" boomed the principal.

"I don't know, sir," mumbled Josh.

"Josh Johnson, do you actually expect me to believe any of this?"

"Um, yes, sir?" said Josh.

The principal banged his desk.

"Well, I don't believe it! I don't believe a word of it! And what's more, we have a zero-tolerance policy for bullying at this school, young man!"

"Bullying? I wasn't bullying, sir! Really! I didn't mean to...I was only..."

The principal leaned forward. His cologne smelled leathery and cowboyish.

"Do you realize that Stacey Hogarth's mother is the head of the Parent Council?" the principal said. "What would she say if I let this infraction go unpunished?"

"I...I don't know, sir," Josh stuttered. "Maybe I could apologize?"

The principal erupted from his chair. He loomed above Josh. The mountain photo with the principal's vow loomed behind him.

"I'm afraid that won't be enough, Mr. Johnson! I'm afraid this merits a three-day suspension."

"A three-day suspension?" Josh gasped. His mother would freak out. She'd think he was turning into a juvenile delinquent.

"Please, sir, can't I do something? I'll clean all the blackboards. I'll mop the floors. I'll sell chocolate bars. I'll do anything. Really, I'm truly sorry."

Principal Hale crossed his arms over his huge chest. He humphed. Finally, his gaze fell on the picture of the men's Olympic hockey team, and his expression softened a little.

"Tell me, son, do you play hockey?" The principal looked down at Josh.

"I'm a pretty good skater," Josh answered hopefully. He'd never played on a hockey team. He wasn't even sure of the rules. But he could skate.

"Fine," said the principal. "I'll tell you what I'll do. As you might have heard, I'm starting a new hockey team for grades five and six. This is a fantastic chance for students to show their school spirit and participate in the Beating Heart of our Culture. Now! I'm looking for players. You come out for the team, and I'll lower your punishment to lunchtime detentions every day this week. How does that sound?"

"Oh, yes, sir! Thank you, sir!" Josh jumped from his chair. He was so relieved at not being suspended, he almost forgot that he didn't know how to play hockey.

"Fine then. First practice today after school." The principal waved his hand at the door, motioning for Josh to leave. Josh scuttled for the exit.

"Oh, and son," Principal Hale called, just as Josh was opening the door.

Josh turned back. "Yes, sir?"

"Better keep your head up. I hear Stacey's got a wicked cross-check." The principal winked. "I reckon she'll be looking to get even."

SEVEN

Enforcer Grrrrl

The recess bell rang as Josh left the principal's office. He rushed to his locker to grab his coat and boots, then ran to the schoolyard filled with hollering kids. His feet skidded on the hard-packed snow as he cut across a soccer game and made for the jungle gym, where Wang hung upside down from the monkey bars. As he got closer, he could see Wilmot sitting on the tire swing and Magnolia leaning against one of the vertical posts. Obviously still intent on playing Nocturnia, Vampire Princess of Doom, Magnolia was dressed in a long black wool cloak and black wool gloves with the fingertips cut off, exposing her long red nails.

She had tiny sparkly jewels on her temples, but the effect was spoiled by her frizzy hair, which sproinged out from beneath her black wool hat. It was hard to take a vampire seriously when she looked as if she'd stuck her finger in an electrical socket.

"What's the scoop, Prez?" Wang flipped down from the frosty metal bars and stuffed his bare hands into his jacket sleeves.

"Principal Hale is a scary guy." Josh sat down on the swing next to Wilmot. The rubber felt cold on his bum. "I got detentions at lunch hour every day this week. And I have to join the hockey team."

"I'm sorry I got you into trouble, Josh." Wilmot hung his head.

"Don't worry, Wil. It's not a big deal."

"But Josh," Magnolia broke in. "What did you find out about the principal? Did you probe his mind? Did you discover his weakness?"

"His mind?" said Josh. "Oh, yeah. Well, he's got hockey posters up on his walls."

"Big surprise," muttered Wilmot.

"And something called the Principal's Vow. With a big picture of a mountain."

"I don't see how that's going to help us," said Magnolia.

"Oh, yeah," said Josh. "And he likes country music."

"Country music?" said Wang, jumping onto the monkey bars again.

"Yeah. There was some song on the radio. Something about tears in a guy's beer and his aching heart and the girl he loved and stuff like that."

"Smoochy music." Magnolia rolled her eyes. "Sheesh!"

"Maybe that's his weakness though," said Wilmot. "You know, country music?"

Josh thought it over. "So if country music is the principal's weakness..."

"I know!" shouted Wang. "We could buy him a horse!"

"A horse?" said Josh.

"It'd be awesome! He could ride it to school."

"No, he couldn't," said Magnolia. "Where would he put it?"

"In the parking lot," said Wang.

"You can't put a horse in the parking lot."

"Why not? It's the same as a car."

"Yeah, except it's got four legs and it poops on things," said Magnolia. "Besides, a horse is too expensive."

"Okay, how about a dog?" said Wang.

"It still costs a lot of money," said Magnolia.

"A chicken!" Wang exclaimed. "We could get him a chicken!"

Wang jumped down from the monkey bars and stuffed his thumbs under his armpits, flapping his elbows like chicken wings.

"*Bok-bok-b'gok!*" Wang clucked. "Chickens are cool."

"But—" said Josh.

"And he could keep it in his office. It wouldn't take up a lot of space."

"He could not," said Magnolia. "Chickens poop on things too."

"We could volunteer to clean it up."

"I am *not* cleaning up chicken poop!"

"Guys! Guys!" Josh wedged himself between them. "I don't think we can get him a live animal." He looked at Wilmot, who was sitting thoughtfully on the tire swing.

"Do you have any ideas, Wil?"

"Well…" Wilmot looked at them, his round face hesitant beneath his dark-green tuque. "You'll probably think it's dumb…"

"Go ahead," said Josh. "Tell us."

"Well, I was thinking…maybe we could write a song."

Magnolia and Wang turned to look at him.

"Just an idea," he mumbled.

"No, it's a good idea," Josh said. "We could write a song to make him change his mind."

"A song that tugs at his heartstrings!" exclaimed Magnolia.

"Headcase could help us," suggested Wilmot.

"Who's Headcase?"

"He's a teenager. But he's really nice. He's the guy who gave me the guitar."

"Brilliant plan!" Wang exclaimed.

"We'll call on him after school," Magnolia said as the bell rang to end recess. "Meet here at the jungle gym."

"Operation Rescue Drama and Music must not fail!" Wang ran toward the school doors.

"You guys go on without me," Josh called after him. He felt the responsibility of the presidency weigh on his shoulders as he scuffed toward the door over the hard-packed snow. "I guess I'll be at hockey practice."

The locker room in the hockey arena smelled like a festering heap of grimy underwear. Josh crinkled his nose as he took a seat on the wooden bench and peered down at the plastic milk crate of hockey gear that Principal Hale had provided to each of the players who'd signed up for the hockey team. Beside the crate lay his skates, which he'd run home to pick up during afternoon recess. All around him, kids yacked and jostled each other as they tried on their equipment. Josh reached into his crate and picked through the tangle of body armor: helmet, neckguard, chest protector, elbow pads, jockstrap, shin pads, mouthguard.

"Hey, Russell." Josh turned to the hefty defenseman sitting on the bench next to him. "How come we have to wear all this stuff?"

"Flying pucks," Russell said grimly. "Flying sticks. Flying bodies."

"Oh," said Josh. He was starting to think a three-day suspension might have been an easier punishment than a three-month sentence on the school hockey team.

It took him awhile to figure out how to put everything on, but finally, strapped together from head to toe with Velcro and hockey tape, Josh tottered onto the rink. He felt like an ice-skating armadillo. He could barely see through the cage of his hockey helmet, let alone hear anything. The shouts of Principal Hale directing the warm-up echoed in garbled syllables around the icy rafters.

From what Josh could tell, the other players were a pretty even mix of kids who looked like they knew what they were doing and kids like him, whose only hockey skill was the ability to stand up on a pair of skates. He counted about thirty boys and half a dozen girls. Among the girls was Zahraa from lion-dancing class. And, of course, Stacey Hogarth.

Stacey was wearing a bright-orange jersey with the nickname *Enforcer Grrrrrl* stitched on the back. As the other players circled the ice, practicing their stickhandling and shooting, Stacey zigzagged through the arena like a runaway Zamboni, threatening to knock down anyone who crossed her path. Josh figured he'd better apologize for pulling her ponytail soon, before she flattened him into roadkill. Or icekill. Whatever the right word was in hockey talk. Coach Hale ordered them into a lineup for the first passing drill, and Josh took the opportunity to slide into place behind Stacey.

He tapped her on the shoulder.

"Om fowwy I poff yo haiwa ing kwaff, Fthtathy," he said.

"What?" Stacey looked at him like he'd just stepped off the slow train from Idiotsville.

Josh spat out his mouthguard. "I said, I'm sorry I pulled your hair in class, Stacey."

"Oh, that!" Stacey attempted to toss her hair. The hockey helmet ruined the effect. "Well, everyone knows you're a girl mauler, Josh Johnson!"

"I...what?...I'm not..."

Before he could get another word in, Stacey reached the front of the line and skated away on the passing drill. Josh went next, but it turned out to be less of a passing drill and more of a miss-the-pass-and-chase-the-puck-down-the-ice drill. When he finally circled back into line, Stacey turned to face him.

"Haw km yoah fwems ahnd hewa, Gshofsh?" she said.

"Huh?" Josh panted.

Stacey spat out her mouthguard. "I said, how come your friends aren't here? You know, Wang and Magnolia? And that dweeby new kid, Wilmot?"

"Wil's not dweeby!" said Josh. "He's a nice guy."

"If he's so dweeby, how come you let him into your club?"

"He's not dweeby!"

"He's dweeby!"

"He's not dweeby!"

"You wouldn't let *me* into your club."

"You don't belong in the club, Stacey! It's a club for kids with problems."

"Well, *I* don't have any problems!" Stacey attempted the hair-tossing move again. The helmet bobbled up and down.

"Exactly! That's why you're not…"

Someone poked Josh in the back with a hockey stick. He looked around and realized that the passing drill was over, and the kids were gathering in a circle around Coach Hale. He glided into the circle.

"Your club's lame," Stacey hissed, gliding into place beside him. Her eyes were black behind the cage of her helmet. "I could make it *way* better."

"No, you couldn't!" Josh shot back. It didn't even make sense. How could a club *with* Stacey in it possibly be better than a club *without* Stacey in it? It wasn't logical.

"All right, kids! Listen up!" Coach Hale boomed. He pulled a marker out of his pocket and started drawing blue Xs and arrows on the ice. Some of the kids, who looked like they knew what they were doing, dropped down to one knee in a tight inner circle around the coach. Josh stood with the rest of the kids in a clueless mob around the outside. It would be cool, Josh thought, to be part of the inner circle—not just because he'd look like a real hockey player, but also because he'd actually be able to hear what the coach was saying.

The arena was so cold and empty and echoey that the words coming out of Coach Hale's mouth seemed to stretch and wobble like giant soap bubbles, floating up to the rafters before Josh could grasp them.

"You!" Coach Hale pointed at Josh. "And you!" He pointed at Zahraa. "Offense!"

"You!" He pointed at Stacey. "Defense! Let's go!"

Josh picked up a puck and passed it to Zahraa while Stacey skated away to occupy her turf at the far end of the ice. Obviously, it was some kind of two-on-one drill. Zahraa carried the puck up the center, which gave Josh time to wonder, as he skated parallel to her on the right wing, why Mr. Hale had chosen him to do the drill against Stacey. Was it coincidence? Or was he giving Stacey a chance at payback? Would a principal do something like that? What about the principal's vow? What about helping young minds to grow? If Stacey beaned him, he wouldn't have any mind *left* to grow, Josh thought desperately.

Zahraa passed the puck. Josh tried to speed up to catch it, but the puck sailed past, bounced off the boards and came to rest a few feet in front of him, right next to a blue line that was painted on the ice. Not far away, Stacey stalked between him and the net.

Josh had no idea what he was supposed to do next in the drill. The only strategy he could think of was to grab the puck and get rid of it as soon as possible. He fixed his eyes on the black disk, which goggled up at him from the glaring-white ice surface. He scooped it onto his stick. He took a stride forward. He looked up to find Zahraa for a pass. But when he glanced down again a split second later, the puck wasn't there. Somehow, it had slid off his stick. Josh circled. The puck eyed him mockingly. He glared back at it. He scooped it up. He fixed his eyes on it as he cradled it on the blade of his stick. Where was Zahraa? Where was the net? Was he close enough to take a shot? Josh looked up. No net. Instead, a speeding orange blur, surmounted by a pair of fierce eyeballs, was bearing down on him from less than three feet away and screaming, "AAAAARGH!"

WHAM!

The blur hit him. It was very solid, for a blur. Josh felt as though someone had thumped him in the chest with a telephone pole. For a millisecond he was weightless, flying, floating through the air, then *thud!* He hit the boards and sprawled to the ice, eye-to-eye with the puck.

Josh heard the swish of skate blades. Ice shavings flew in his face. A stick skimmed the ice and plucked the puck from under his nose. The orange blur hovered over him. "Dweeb!" shouted Stacey's voice. The skates swished away and Josh was left lying alone in the cold.

He thought about Wang, Wilmot and Magnolia. He thought about them sitting together somewhere in a warm room, writing a country song for Principal Hale. He wished he could be there with them. Country music might be painful, with its tears and beers and aching hearts. But it couldn't possibly be as painful as school hockey.

EIGHT

Cousin Willy and the Wang Dang Doodles

"You're killin' me, little dude," said Headcase. He plucked a string on his Fender Stratocaster guitar and pressed the distortion pedal to send the note warping around the basement.

"Please!" Wilmot shouted. "You've got to help us!"

Headcase let the note die out, and then he flopped into the orange-and-gold armchair.

"Country music? Tell me you're kidding me, little dude. No, wait—tell me it's a nightmare and I'm gonna wake up from it any minute."

Headcase squeezed his eyes shut, smacked one hand over his face, took a deep breath, let it out and opened his eyes again.

"Was it a nightmare, little dude? Is it over now?"

"No." Wilmot gulped. "I'm really sorry, but we need your help to write a country music song."

Wilmot, Wang and Magnolia were crammed into a small area of open space between the stereo equipment, Headcase's Rock Through the Ages music collection and a used drum kit that he'd set up recently for when his friends came over to jam. Sitting cross-legged on the grungy brown carpet, Wilmot looked up imploringly at Headcase. Apart from the orange-and-gold armchair, there was no furniture in the basement. "Furniture? Waste of valuable floor space, dudes," Headcase had told them.

Lounging in the chair with his feet slung over the armrest, Headcase looked at Wilmot and shook his head.

"Okay, little dude," he said. "Explain this to me one more time."

Wilmot turned to Magnolia. Maybe she could explain it. She was good at explaining things, and besides, she had a way of getting people on her side. But Magnolia waved at him to go ahead. Wilmot picked a bit of brown fuzz off the carpet and rolled it between his thumb and forefinger.

"Well," he began. "See, the principal canceled the school music program."

"And drama," Magnolia broke in.

Wilmot fumbled to a stop. Did she want him to tell the story, or didn't she?

"Sorry, Wil," said Magnolia. "Go ahead."

"Okay. Anyway," Wilmot continued, "he canceled the Drama and Music program. And so how am I going to learn guitar? Because my dad isn't going to pay for lessons. I mean, he'd flip out if he even knew I *had* a guitar. He's this totally smart math professor and he says he needs silence to concentrate. And I'm supposed to be working harder on chess and on my homework, so I can get smart like him.

"So anyway, we decided we had to change the principal's mind. Then Josh found out—he's not here, but he's a friend of ours—anyway, he found out that the principal likes country music. So, we thought…we thought…" Wilmot fumbled. What had they thought? That by writing a country song they could change the principal's mind, convince him to cancel the hockey team and bring back Drama and Music? Now that Wilmot tried to put it into words, it sounded like a dumb scheme.

"We thought," Magnolia broke in, "that the power of the music would stir the principal's soul! That his heart would swell, and he would realize that life is meaningless without drama and song!"

The three kids fell silent, waiting for Headcase's reaction.

The teenager strummed thoughtfully on the guitar.

"It's a noble cause, little dudes. But I gave my soul to rock 'n' roll. Country music? No way. Can't do it. Sorry."

Headcase riffed off a series of complicated hard-rock chords. The music burned into Wilmot's heart.

"You wouldn't have to play," he pleaded. "You'd just have to help us write a song."

"Uh-uh, little dude. I told you, Headcase is a rock 'n' roller." He held up his fist with the index and pinkie sticking out. "Born to rock, little dude. Born. To. Rock."

Magnolia stood up.

"But you don't have to be Headcase," she argued. "You can be someone else. It's like in a play. Like acting a part. Forget Headcase. What if you were...let me think...what if you were Cousin Les?"

"Who's Cousin Les?"

"Cousin Les?" Magnolia tapped her fingers together. "Cousin Les is a harmonica player from Mooseberry,

Saskatchewan. And Wilmot..." She turned to him. "He isn't Wilmot anymore. He's cousin Willy."

"Cousin Willy?" said Wilmot.

"A country guitar player."

"What about me?" Wang jumped to his feet.

"Wang? You're..." Magnolia paused.

"You're Wang Dang Doodle, man," said Headcase.

"Wang Dang Doodle?"

"Classic tune by Howlin' Wolf. Google it. Great guitar part." Headcase played a riff, three low notes and a high twang: *ba ba bow yeeeow!*

"Cool," said Magnolia. "So that's our band. Cousin Willy and the Wang Dang Doodles. Now all we need to do is write the song."

"Hold on a minute, little dudette," said Headcase. "I'll help you on one condition: no one ever finds out that Headcase wrote a country song. If you ever tell anyone, I put the Curse of the Guitar Gods on all of you."

Headcase made the rock 'n' roll symbol again, and this time he jabbed his index and pinkie fingers toward Wilmot like a pitchfork.

"The Curse of the Guitar Gods?" Wilmot shrunk back.

"Your hands cripple up like this!" Headcase bent his fingers into a claw. "And you can never play guitar again. Ever!"

"I won't tell anyone! I swear!"

"Yeah, we swear!" Magnolia and Wang added.

"Okay little dudes, I trust you." Headcase let his hand relax. "Now, what was the name of your principal?"

"Mr. Hale," said Magnolia.

Headcase strummed a few chords. "'The Ballad of Principal Hale,'" he said. "What rhymes with *Hale*?"

"I know!" cried Wang. "How about, he's slimy like a snail?"

Magnolia crossed her arms. "It's supposed to be nice stuff, Wang!"

"Blubbery like a whale?"

"Wang!"

"But it's true…"

"I have an idea," Wilmot piped up. "How about something like, riding a lonesome trail?"

"Hey, that's good!" Magnolia exclaimed. "Really cowboyish."

Headcase plucked a few chords and sighed.

"You've got talent, little dude," he said. "Too much talent to waste on country music."

NINE

The Lion's Promise

The next Saturday morning, Wang invited Josh over to his place after lion-dance class.

"I guess I could come over for a bit," Josh said. But he seemed to have something on his mind, as they dodged along the sidewalk, climbing up the snowbanks and scooting beneath the tables of fresh vegetables and dry, salted fish set out by the Chinatown grocers at the outdoor market. At last they reached Wang's parents' store and set foot inside to the tinkle of the entrance bell. Wang dragged Josh into an aisle of canned goods before his mother could spot him and put him to work.

"Want to see something cool?" he asked.

"Sure," said Josh.

"Come on. Follow me!"

Keeping an eye out for his parents, Wang led the way to a narrow wooden door at the back of the store and then down a set of steep wooden stairs into the basement storage room. He swung his hand around until it hit the chain on the lightbulb that hung from the ceiling. He gave a yank and the bulb lit up the room's bumpy, gray stone walls, which were covered by a grid of rough wooden shelves. Boxes and cans, all labeled in Chinese characters, filled most of the space. But on one high-up shelf, the cans of bamboo shoots and pickled ginger had been cleared away to make room for something much more precious.

Hui Bing's lion costume.

The jewels on the horn of the lion's head sparkled in the light of the bare bulb. The lion's tufted ears seemed to perk up and listen to Wang and Josh while the brilliant eyes looked down upon them with a mixture of majestic strength and laughter, as if to say, "I am the king. Come and make merry with me."

"Wow!" said Josh. "What's it doing here?"

"Master Hui Bing has a small apartment. He asked my parents to take care of it for him until he finds a bigger place."

"Cool," said Josh. He reached up toward the glossy red paint of the lion's face and the white fur on its chin, but it was out of reach.

"I don't think we're supposed to touch it," said Wang. "Not until we're chosen for the dance."

Josh nodded and sat down on the bottom step of the narrow staircase, his bum fitting into the groove worn by years of footsteps. He looked preoccupied and a little glum. Maybe because he wasn't one of the better dancers in the class, Wang thought.

"Want me to practice some moves with you?" Wang asked.

"Nah," said Josh. He looked up. "I hate to tell you this, Wang, but I don't think we've got a chance."

"That's not true. You just have to practice some more," said Wang. "Hey, watch this!"

Wang had been itching to try out a trick that he'd seen in a really cool movie, *The Kung Fu Swordsman of the Jade Mountain*. The move started with a running leap at a wall. You planted one foot on the wall, took another step straight up the wall, flipped over backward and landed with both feet planted flat on the floor. It was amazing in the movie, where Kung Fu master Jiang Cheng executed the move while twirling double-bladed swords in both hands, cutting off the heads of two enemy warriors.

Although the storage room was small, it had one bare wall, and Wang felt juiced up enough to try the move. Maybe it would pull Josh out of his funk. He ran at the wall, leaped up and planted one foot on it. For a split second he hung in the air, perfectly horizontal. Then the force of gravity jerked him earthward, and he thudded onto his back on the concrete floor.

"Ow," said Josh. "Are you okay?"

Wang looked up. A black blob floated before his eyes, dotted with multicolored pinpricks of light. He blinked a few times. Josh's face shimmered into focus.

"I can do it," Wang wheezed. "I just need more of a running start."

"For sure," said Josh. "But seriously, Wang, I'm afraid you're not gonna get the part."

"What are you talking about, Josh?" Wang turned his head. It hurt to move, but he didn't think he'd broken anything. Gingerly, he touched the back of his head. No blood. That was a good sign.

"You know how I was late for class again today?" Josh said. "Al Tung was in the change room talking to another guy. And he said him and his brother Shawn were getting the parts. For sure."

"That's crazy," said Wang, the floor cold against his back. "Those guys can't dance."

"Yeah, but you know when Larry got back from China? Well, he didn't have very much money. So Al and Shawn's dad rented him an apartment, really cheap. So now he kind of owes them a favor. That's what Al said anyway."

"That's not right!" Wang felt dizzy.

Josh shrugged. "That's what I heard."

"I don't believe it," said Wang.

"I don't know," said Josh. "Anyway, I should get going. My mom wanted me to be home for lunch."

Josh headed up the stairs, but Wang didn't move from his spot on the storage-room floor. *Give the dance parts to Al and Shawn Tung?* Master Hui Bing would never do such a thing. He'd promised to hold a fair competition. He'd promised that the best dancers would win. He'd said that the lion himself would choose the winners.

Wang looked at the magnificent lion high above him as though he were lying in the grass and looking up at the clouds. He'd never been to China, but his mother had told him many of the old folktales, and when he looked at the lion, the stone walls of the basement storage room seemed to transform themselves into the snowcapped Huangshan mountains. Through a blue mist, he seemed to hear the far-off gongs of the emperor's court, and he remembered his mother's tale of how the emperor dreamed of being rescued from his enemies by a mythical lion, and how he commanded that a ceremonial lion dance be created in honor of this auspicious dream.

The lion symbolized prosperity and bravery and good fortune. It didn't symbolize getting cheap rent on an apartment! Master Hui Bing would never betray the lion in that way.

Would he?

Wang gazed up at the lion. The lion gazed back at him. Wang sighed and heaved himself to his feet. He turned away from the lion with a heavy heart. But as he set his foot on the well-worn wooden staircase, Wang seemed to hear a deep, shaggy voice inside his head.

"The lion shall dance for a noble cause," said the voice. "The dancer shall know when he is chosen."

TEN

The Ballad of Principal Hale

The end of January brought a week of warm, blue-sky weather. Streams of melting snow trickled down the sidewalks, and the sun glinted off the icicles that dripped from the eaves of every roof. It was the perfect time for the world premiere of Cousin Willy and the Wang Dang Doodles, Magnolia thought with satisfaction.

It had taken a lot of work to get here—and learning the song was only half of it. In the quest for perfect costumes, Magnolia had dragged Wilmot and Wang to every thrift store in town until they were kitted out in cowboy hats, leather boots, jeans and jean jackets.

She'd found a tambourine with leather tassels for Wang, since Headcase wouldn't let them move his drum set out of his apartment. For herself, she had chosen a flouncy red-and-white-checkered skirt with a matching red jacket and red-and-white-checkered hair bows.

Now, standing in the morning light on the sidewalk outside of Mocha Mo's Coffee to Go, Magnolia felt that Cousin Willy and the Wang Dang Doodles were as ready as they'd ever be for their musical debut.

"Where should I plug this in?" Wang asked as he struggled up the sidewalk, carrying the old amplifier that Headcase had loaned them.

"Mo said we could use the outlet in his store," said Magnolia. Wang disappeared inside the coffee shop just as Wilmot arrived, clutching his guitar and looking nervous. It was amazing how the kid could break into a sweat even in the middle of winter, Magnolia reflected. Sweating on demand would be a useful skill for an actor. Especially in a horror movie, if you were being chased by a monster. It was so difficult in those situations to project *authentic* emotion.

"Are you sure he's coming?" Wilmot asked.

"Josh says the principal picks up a coffee at Mocha Mo's every Thursday morning after hockey practice," said Magnolia.

"Gotta trust the prez," chipped in Wang, arriving back on the sidewalk. "He's our inside informant."

"I guess so." Wilmot plucked a tentative-sounding note. "I wish I was a better guitar player. Headcase only taught me three chords."

"Relax," said Magnolia. "You only need three chords. This is country music, not Beethoven, remember?"

"But—"

"Shh! Guys!" Wang pointed down the street. "Here he comes!"

Magnolia plugged the guitar into the amp as the tall barrel-chested form of Principal Hale came striding down the sidewalk. He turned in to Mocha Mo's and came out a few minutes later with a large coffee cup in hand.

"Wait until he's settled," Magnolia whispered as Principal Hale lowered his large rear end onto the bench outside the coffee shop, yawned and took the first sip from his cup.

Magnolia switched on her microphone. "Okay, boys," she whooped. "Hit it!"

Wilmot launched into the opening chords of "The Ballad of Principal Hale." Wang shook his tambourine. Magnolia raised her voice and sang.

All over Oakview Public School, the folks all tell a tale
About a brave and honest man whose name is
  Principal Hale!
He's handsome, bold and true
And the kids all love him too!
Principal Hale! Oh, Principal Hale!

Principal Hale raised his eyebrows. Sipping his coffee, he turned his attention toward the band. Magnolia sang on.

Principal Hale! Oh, Principal Hale!
Like a cowboy riding on a lonesome trail!
When a student breaks a rule,
He kicks him right out of school!
He sends him to jail! Oh, Principal Hale!

Principal Hale smiled. His foot began tapping. Magnolia belted out the third verse.

And when a food fight breaks out in the caf-e-te-ri-a,
Or when a gunky spitball causes mass hys-te-ri-a,
Principal Hale is sent
To protect the in-no-cent
He'll never fail! Oh, Principal Hale!

Magnolia snuck a glance at Wilmot. He was concentrating intently on the chord changes, eyes glued to his fingers, strumming and sweating but somehow making it through without a mistake. The principal nodded and stamped along in time. Magnolia launched into the final chorus:

Principal Hale! Oh, Principal Hale!
He's as mighty as a great Atlantic whale!
He'll defend our noble school,
Down to the last mo-le-cule,
He's an alpha male! Oh, Principal Hale!

Magnolia held the last note for emphasis. With a flourish, Wilmot strummed the final chord. Principal Hale set his coffee cup down on the bench and applauded.

"That was a fine song, kids! Just fine!"

"Oh, thank you, sir!" Magnolia stepped forward and dropped into a curtsy. "I'm Magnolia, sir, and this is my cousin Willy."

Wilmot tipped his hat.

"And that's my cousin Wang over there."

Wang shook his tambourine.

"Yippee-ki-yay!" Wang yodelled. "Git along, little dogie!"

"Um, nice to meet you, Cousin Wang," said the principal. "Tell me, did you kids come up with that song yourselves?"

"Oh, yes, sir!" Magnolia replied. "Because you see, we were hoping..."

She stopped, letting her voice catch in her throat, looked up to the sky and let out a sob.

"But, no! It will never happen!"

Magnolia flung herself down on the bench beside the principal and, with a mighty effort of dramatic willpower, burst into tears.

She peeked at the principal from between her fingers. He looked bewildered.

"Now, now, little miss." He patted her awkwardly on the shoulder. "I'm sure it can't be that bad. Why don't you tell me all about it?"

Magnolia wiped her eyes and gazed up at him.

"You see, sir, our parents are all too poor to send us to music lessons. Everything that we know about music, we learned at our own humble kitchen table. We just want to keep improving and become the best country musicians in the land. Right, boys?" She turned to Wilmot and Wang.

"Yeppers," said Cousin Willy.

"Dang tootin'," said Cousin Wang.

"That's why we were hoping..." Magnolia sniffed. "We were hoping that you might find it in your heart to bring back the school Drama and Music program."

Magnolia gave the principal her best puppy-dog eyes. The principal's face turned red. He let out an embarrassed cough. He scratched the back of his neck.

"Well, unfortunately, kids, the fact is that—well, that money has been allocated for another worthy program this year."

Magnolia broke down in tears.

"Oh, my heart is breaking!" she sobbed. "My dreams are shattered! My life is not worth living!"

"There, there," said the principal, patting her on the shoulder again.

Wilmot stepped forward.

"Please, sir," he said earnestly. "Isn't there anything you can do?"

The principal scratched the back of his neck again. He looked at the faces of the kids, and slowly he nodded.

"I'll tell you what I'll do, kids. I'm planning a big hockey game soon. The Principal's Challenge Cup. We'll be playing against our crosstown rivals, the Kilborn Killers. I'm giving the whole school the afternoon off to attend the game. You put a little show together, five or six songs, and I'll make sure you get a chance to play at the intermission. How does that sound?"

"Oh, yes, sir!" cried Magnolia, wiping her eyes. "Thank you, sir."

The principal patted her once more on the shoulder. He picked up his coffee cup and rose from the bench. "Good stuff! I'll be looking forward to your show," he said jovially.

Magnolia watched as he sauntered off, kicking up his heels and singing to himself, *"Principal Hale! Oh, Principal Hale! He's perfect right down to his big toenail!"*

She turned toward the boys. "Sheesh! That guy sure is full of himself!"

Wang threw his arm around Wilmot's shoulders. "You were great, Wil!" he said. "Did you hear that? We've got a show!"

He flung his cowboy hat in the air. "Yippee-ki-yay!"

"Yeah, but..." said Wilmot.

Wang's cowboy hat fell down and beaned Wilmot in the nose. "Sorry," said Wang. He picked up the hat, shook it off and set it on his head.

Wilmot rubbed his nose.

"Yeah, but the Drama and Music program is still canceled."

"Don't worry, Wil," said Magnolia. "We're gonna put on such a great show that he'll have to bring it back!"

"Yeah," said Wang. "We're gonna be awesome!"

The street, which had been nearly deserted when they'd started playing, was now filling up with kids hurrying toward school, knapsacks bumping against their backs.

"Better pack up or we're going to be late," said Magnolia.

"You really think we're going to be awesome?" said Wilmot.

"Totally awesome," said Wang.

ELEVEN

I Wanna Rock!

Wilmot bounced up the stairs to Headcase's front porch, swinging his guitar case and humming "The Ballad of Principal Hale." *Totally awesome*. Wang had said his performance was *totally awesome*. He couldn't remember the last time he'd done anything *totally awesome*. His feet tingled in his cowboy boots. He felt as though he'd grown three inches taller that day. All during school, he'd barely been able to sit still at his desk, bursting with the news of their upcoming performance. He looked back impatiently at Magnolia and Wang, lugging the heavy amplifier up the walkway.

"C'mon, you guys!" he called. At last his friends reached the top of the stairs, and Wilmot, setting his cowboy hat at a jaunty angle, rang the doorbell.

The door swung open. Headcase stood there in bare feet, acid-washed jeans and a black T-shirt emblazoned with a flying death skull.

"Cowboy costumes?" He groaned. "Tell me I'm hallucinating, little dudes."

"You should've seen us," Wilmot exclaimed. "We were totally awesome!"

"Yeah!" chipped in Wang, shaking his tambourine. "The principal wants us to play at a hockey game. Can you believe it? Five or six songs, he said."

"Five or six songs? You're losing your minds, little dudes."

"So we've gotta start rehearsing," continued Wilmot. "We only have about a month to practice."

Headcase stared at them. He blew a strand of stringy brown hair out of his eyes.

"So, can we come in?" Wilmot asked.

"More country music?" asked Headcase.

"It's the principal's favorite."

"Sorry, little dudes. If you ain't rockin', don't bother knockin'. "

Kate Jaimet

Headcase turned away and gave the door a tap with his foot to swing it shut. Wilmot felt like he'd been kicked in the teeth. It wasn't fair, cutting them down when they'd just gotten their first gig! He stuck his foot in the doorway before the lock could catch and pushed the door open.

"Wait!" he called at the shaggy mane of hair retreating down the hallway.

Headcase turned. "What?"

"It's just that…"

"Oh, Headcase!" cried Magnolia behind him. "It's just that you're our only hope!"

Flouncy skirt rustling, Magnolia pushed past Wilmot, swept into the narrow hallway and fell to her knees on the slushy floor.

"Oh, please!" She clasped her hands to her chest. "The song you wrote was so powerful! It melted the principal's heart. He's giving us a chance! We can't let it slip away! Don't you see? We need you!"

Headcase shook his head. "We had a bargain, little dudette. One country song. Only one."

"But Cousin Les…"

"Cousin Les is dead. Dead like disco."

He turned his back on them again. Nothing came into Wilmot's head, no words he could say to change the teenager's mind. He felt like a cowboy who'd been bonked over the head with a tin of beans. But just as Headcase's back began to disappear down the basement staircase, Wilmot heard the jangle of a tambourine, felt another body push past him and saw Wang, in a flash of denim and leather, leap over Magnolia's head and land in front of her in the hallway.

"After him!" shouted Wang.

"After him!" shouted Magnolia, scrambling to her feet.

"After him!" shouted Wilmot.

Madly they rushed down the narrow, dark, rickety staircase into the rock 'n' roll sanctuary of Headcase's basement.

"You can't do this!" Wang's words tumbled out of him as he pounded down the stairs. "It's our only chance to save the Drama and Music program! It's a noble cause! You said so yourself! We must fight for the noble cause! All for one and one for all! The stream springs from the heart of the mountain, but who knows the heart of the lonely rutabaga!"

Reaching the bottom of the staircase, Wang jumped with a flourish onto the grungy basement rug.

"You're crazy, Wang Dang Doodle," said Headcase.

"Please!" Wilmot squeezed past Wang and grabbed Headcase's arm. "It's only one concert. And besides, you don't have to play, you just have to teach us. And no one's gonna know because we're not gonna tell anyone—we promise. It's not that bad, and besides…"

"Forsake your entreaties, young friend!" A voice both soft and powerful emerged from the gloom of the basement. "Your supplications are in vain! He has committed his life to the Path of Rock and Roll."

Wilmot fell silent. He peered around the dim room. Aside from the red spotlight that fell on Headcase's Vintage Hot Rod '57 Fender Stratocaster, the only illumination came from a pale trickle of winter sunlight that seeped through the tiny windows high up in the walls. At first Wilmot could see no living thing among the array of black-and-chrome stereo equipment. But finally he spotted, curled in the depths of Headcase's orange-and-gold armchair, a pale, thin, gauzy girl with long white-blond hair.

The girl wore a silken gown the color of moonlight on water lilies.

"My girlfriend, Freya," said Headcase. He waved at her, then back at them. "This is little dude, little dudette and Wang Dang Doodle."

"I am honored to meet you," Freya breathed. The words floated from her mouth as though exhaled on puffs of cloud.

"Hey," said Wilmot and Wang together.

"Cool costume," said Magnolia.

The girl stroked her dress. "It is the garb of my people, the Nymphenfolk of Sussrumnir."

"Awesome," said Wang. "Hey, Magnolia! You should show her Nocturnia, Vampire Princess of Doom!"

"Halt!" The girl shuddered as she held up one pale and slender hand. "The vampires are the sworn enemies of my people. Long ago, when the gods still feasted in Valhalla, I possessed the enchantments to ward them away. But alas! I have lost my powers since I assumed this mortal form."

"Is she for real?" Magnolia muttered.

Wilmot gave a baffled shrug.

"I have sought to learn their secrets by study of this ancient tome," continued the girl. From behind a cushion, she drew out a hardcover book with the title *Vampirology* in Gothic script on the front. On the back cover, a bright orange sticker said *Bargain Bin! 99 Cents!*

"Much wisdom is contained therein," Freya declared.

"Cool," said Wang.

Magnolia crossed her arms. She seemed upset at being upstaged by a reincarnated Viking fairy.

"That's great, that you're learning how to defeat the vampires and everything," she said, "but I don't see how it's going to help us with Principal Hale."

"Little dudes, since you followed me down here, at least take my advice," broke in Headcase. "Forget about this honky-tonk principal. Play for your fans."

Headcase loped over to the guitar stand, picked up his instrument and let loose a hard-driving riff: *bum ba duh-na-na duh-na-na-naaaaaah.*

He held the last note, working the distortion pedal to send the sound wave shivering around the bare brick walls.

"Cool," whispered Wilmot.

"Play for your fans," Headcase said.

"But," Wilmot objected, "we don't have any fans. Except the principal."

Headcase let the note die out.

"Little dude! How many kids are coming to this hockey game?"

"I dunno. The whole school, I guess."

"You think the whole school wants to hear country music?"

"But it's the principal's favorite."

"Listen, little dude. Are you gonna be a victim of authority or are you gonna rock 'n' roll?"

"But what if the principal hates it?"

"Doesn't matter, little dude."

"But—"

"Don't you get it, Wil?" Magnolia broke in. "He means, if we really rock, the school's going to love us so much that the principal will *have* to bring back the Drama and Music program! Right?"

"You got it, little dudette," said Headcase.

"It's a cunning plan!" Wang exclaimed.

"But what if he doesn't? What if he hates it? What if he never lets us play again?"

"Then you go out in a blaze of glory, little dude," Headcase said.

He let rip a C chord.

"You wave the banner of rock and roll!"

He sent an F chord shrieking after the C.

"You fight for the right to party!"

He burned the air with a fiery G chord.

"And if you go down, you go down fighting! 'Cause it's better to burn out than to fade away, little dudes!"

Headcase closed his eyes, threw back his head and strafed the room with a rapid-fire blast of notes.

Sharp as spikes, the chords flew from his guitar, piercing the air with the screeching sound of heavy metal.

Better to burn out than to fade away. Wilmot remembered all the times he'd felt like he was fading away—all those hopeless chess tournaments under the glaring eyes of his father, where every move he made was wrong, where his pieces disappeared one by one from the board, where he could feel himself sliding toward checkmate, being obliterated, turning into nothing. Headcase was right. It was better to burn out than to fade away.

Wilmot pumped his fist in the air.

"I wanna rock!" he shouted.

Wang threw a flying karate kick and landed beside him.

"I wanna rock!" he screamed.

Wilmot flung his head up and down, thrashing an air guitar. Wang leaped up and landed in the splits on the floor. Earsplitting heavy-metal music shot through every crack and cranny of the room. Magnolia ripped her cowboy hat from her head and threw it in a corner.

"I wanna rock!" she screamed.

And Freya, silent in the depths of her armchair, held up her tiny fist with her pinkie and index fingers outstretched in the universal symbol of rock 'n' roll.

TWELVE

Dekey-J

February brought snow and cold weather and a long series of tough days in Josh's life. Every Thursday morning, he trudged through the empty streets to hockey practice, the pale sun casting no warmth in the washed-out winter sky. He had never felt so bruised and battered, so beat-up and beaten down, as he did that season on the Oakview Overachievers hockey team.

The hockey team was supposed to be recreational and non-contact. But try telling that to Principal Hale. "You can't help a little incidental contact, ha ha ha!" he'd say as the bigger kids plowed down the smaller kids and the smaller kids ducked and dodged for their lives. Since the school league for grades-five-and-six hockey was new that year, some of the referees didn't realize there was a non-contact rule either. The players could tell after about thirty seconds on the ice whether the ref was going to call a penalty on body contact. If not, the game became a free-for-all, with the bruisers terrorizing the smaller kids, and the fanatical hockey parents screaming in the stands. Josh, one of the smaller kids, skated through his shifts in constant danger of being blindsided by a human wrecking ball on ice skates. Luckily, he was fast enough to avoid most of the other players, so fast that the coach gave him the nickname "Dekey-J."

Get rid of the puck; that was Dekey-J's motto. Get rid of it fast. That way, no one could bodycheck him, and he wouldn't have to carry the puck up the ice—a skill he hadn't gotten the hang of anyway. Every time he managed to pick up the puck on his stick, it slid off the blade like a pat of butter off a hot knife. How was he supposed to keep it there while he skated forward? It didn't make any sense. In other sports with sticks, you just whacked the ball and that was it. Baseball. Tennis. Badminton. Ping-Pong. Golf. Did golf players run down the field, knocking the ball along with their putters? Of course not. It was ridiculous. Hockey was like some kind of crazy egg-and-spoon race on skates, where the other racers were allowed to smash into you and steal your egg. Josh wasn't any better at lion dancing than he was at hockey, but at least the lion dancers didn't slew-foot each other or ram their competitors into the boards.

It was pretty clear where all the money from the Drama and Music program was going: the team rented extra weekend ice time for practices and took bus trips to out-of-town games. Every game, Josh would come home a little more pounded and pummeled. He would have been happy to quit the hockey team. He felt that his many bumps and bruises more than paid for the little yank he'd given to Stacey's ponytail. But there was one problem: he couldn't leave Stacey alone with Principal Hale.

Stacey had come up with the dumb idea of getting a bunch of her friends together to perform a spirit rally at the Principal's Challenge Cup game. But when she'd talked to Principal Hale about it, he'd told her he couldn't fit it in because Cousin Willy and the Wang Dang Doodles were going to perform instead. Ever since then, she'd been trying to get Principal Hale to change his mind. Josh had to stay on the team so he could stick close to Principal Hale and remind him how hard the band was working on the show and how much he was going to love it.

His only comfort was that he'd managed to avoid any major injuries. That is, until the third week in February.

It started off as an ordinary Thursday-morning practice. Maybe they would just do passing and shooting drills, Josh thought hopefully, as he layered himself into his hockey equipment and skated onto the rink.

But instead, Coach Hale called for a scrimmage.

"Show me your stuff, Dekey-J!" Coach Hale boomed, slapping Josh on the back as he positioned him on the right wing, directly opposite Stacey Hogarth.

"Yeah, Dekey-J," taunted Stacey. "Show me your stuff!"

The whistle blew, and the kid in the center passed the puck to Josh. Josh missed the pass and the puck kept going, skimming over the ice toward the boards. Josh knew he had to chase it down, but that put him on a collision course with Stacey, who was already skating hard toward it. Luckily, Josh was the faster skater. He zipped to the puck, reached it just as it bounced off the boards and whacked it down the ice. With Stacey bearing down on him, Josh circled to the left and dodged out of her way.

Ker-smash! Stacey went flying into the boards, hit them full-force, lost her balance and landed on her rump on the ice.

"Nice move, Dekey-J!" Coach Hale shouted from the bench.

But Josh knew that from that moment on, Stacey would be out for blood.

Stacey came at him from the right. She came at him from the left. She came at him when he had the puck. She came at him when he didn't have the puck. She came at him on offense, defense and in the neutral zone. She came at him on face-offs and shift changes. Josh gave up all hope of actually playing a game of hockey. All he wanted to do was survive the scrimmage with all his body parts intact. When the buzzer sounded for the last two minutes of play, Josh breathed a sigh of relief.

Only 120 seconds left in the game.

Stacey's team pushed the puck deep into Josh's offensive zone. They were putting pressure on the net, scrapping in the corners, firing shots at the goalie. Josh knew that the confusion provided the perfect scenario for Stacey to shove him into the boards or swipe him with a dirty slew foot. Escaping from the pack of players, Josh skated to the open ice in the neutral zone, where he hung back from the action, saving his skin while he watched the seconds tick down.

Then, with a minute still left on the clock, a defenseman shot the puck out of the zone and it came directly to Josh, standing all alone at center ice.

Josh caught the puck on his stick. He turned to face the opposite goal. Zahraa stood guarding the net. There was no one between them. He felt a sudden surge of adrenaline. This was his chance for a breakaway!

Slowly at first, but gaining speed with each stride, he charged toward the opposite goal. He felt the smoothness of his skate blades cutting across the ice, the buzz of the cold air in his ears. He saw the target ahead of him, felt the weight of the puck on his stick. He knew he could do it. He knew he could score! He drew back his stick to shoot.

Wham!

Something hit him from behind.

It hit him with such force that it sent him flying off his skates, crashing headfirst into the goalpost. His helmet slipped off his head and he felt the post give way as the net went skidding off its moorings. He lurched forward, his skate blade touching the rink, then slipping out from under him as he fell and cracked his forehead against the cold, hard ice.

Josh tasted blood.

"Are you okay?"

Zahraa knelt beside him.

Josh sat up. He couldn't see out of his right eye. He was too dazed to speak.

"Oh my gosh!" Zahraa exclaimed. "What happened to your face?"

Josh reached up. Above his right eye, he felt a bump forming.

Coach Hale helped him up and took him to the dressing room. He gave Josh an ice pack and gave Stacey a five-minute penalty and a lecture about illegal cross-checking. It wasn't much comfort, though, as Josh looked in the grimy locker-room mirror and saw his right eye turning as black as a bruised banana.

But if that February was full of dark days for Josh, Wilmot was having the time of his life.

THIRTEEN

Sign of a Vampire

Every Tuesday morning, Wilmot snuck out of the house before his parents woke up and smuggled his guitar to school. On those frosty mornings when the smoke rose in white wisps from the chimneys and the sky glowed pale in the winter sunlight, Wilmot walked to school the long way, killing time—crunching his boots through the ice on the sidewalk puddles, blowing out his breath in puffs of smoke, replaying the songs he'd learned from Headcase over and over again in his head. And every Tuesday after school—the one day Headcase didn't have to go to his job at a grocery warehouse—the Dunces gathered in Headcase's basement to jam, Wilmot on guitar, Magnolia on vocals and Wang thrashing away on the drums. "Play as loud as you want, Wang Dang Doodle," Headcase told him. "But whatever you do, don't lose the beat."

Headcase had already taught Wilmot the basic chords. Now they moved on to more advanced chords and picking. Wilmot found that, unlike chess, the guitar came easily to him. Soon he could tell what chords Headcase was playing just by listening, and he could copy the tunes on his own guitar.

Every Tuesday evening, Wilmot smuggled the guitar back into his house through the laundry room. His mom was impressed with how he'd taken responsibility for sorting the laundry. And when his dad asked why he was coming home so late after school on Tuesdays—sometimes as late as six or six thirty—he told him he was hanging out with Wang from the chess club. It wasn't exactly a lie. Wang was in the chess club. It's just that what they did on Tuesday afternoons had nothing whatsoever to do with chess.

On weekends, and sometimes even on weekdays, Wilmot would set his alarm for 1:00 AM so that he could wake up and practice while his parents were sleeping. In the dead of night, with the moonlight streaming through his window, he would kneel on the cold wood floor, pull the cardboard sweater box out from under his bed, lift the lid and take out his shining, black guitar with the red thunderbolts. He would climb back up on the bed, wrapping his warm blanket around him—his father always turned down the heat at night to save energy—and he'd practice chord shifts with his left hand, strumming or picking softly with his right. His nose and fingertips would be prickling with cold by the time he stowed the guitar back in its sweater box. He only allowed himself to play for one hour a night. If he showed up too tired at the breakfast table, his parents would get suspicious. But as he tucked himself back into bed, the music would play on and on in his head, and often it would still be playing when he woke again in the light of morning.

Then one Tuesday afternoon, disaster struck.

That Tuesday, as usual, Wilmot walked to Headcase's apartment after school with Wang and Magnolia. He rang the bell and stood on the front porch, tossing around some lyrics to their new "Rock Anthem for Principal Hale" with Wang. But the moment the door swung open, he sensed something was wrong.

There was something sad about the door that day. It wasn't just the chipped paint and the grime around the handle. No, it was the listless way it swung open,

as though swinging were barely worth the effort.
And behind the door stood Headcase. He looked as
though he'd been chewed up and spat out. His eyes
were red. His hair straggled down around his face.
The long sleeves of his AC/DC hoodie were streaked
with nose-wipe.

"It's all over, little dudes."

"What?" said Wang, Wilmot and Magnolia together.

"She left me," Headcase said. "And she ripped out
my heart."

Headcase leaned against the grimy wall of the
hallway and slid down it until his bum hit the puddle
of slush and road salt on the floor. He didn't seem to
care. He buried his head in his hands. His long, tangled
hair hung over his face like someone's failed string-art
project.

"Love hurts, little dudes," he said. "Love hurts."

Wilmot looked at Wang. Wang looked at Magnolia.
Together, they sat down next to Headcase on the dirty
hallway floor.

"What happened?" Magnolia said gently.

Without speaking, Headcase pried off one of his
sneakers and peeled away the sock.

He held his foot up. It was a pale, bony foot, and it
stank like a dog who'd rolled in dead squirrel, but Wilmot

couldn't see why it would make a girl break up with a guy. Couldn't he just wash it?

Headcase spread his toes. They were joined together by thin flaps of skin.

"Webbed feet?" said Magnolia.

"Yeah," said Headcase.

"What's the problem?" said Magnolia. "My dad's got webbed feet. It's a genetic whatchamacallum. You know, you get it from your parents."

"Like bat's wings." Headcase flapped his foot. "Sign of a vampire. That's what it says in her book."

He lowered his head in his hands and let out a sniff.

"She thinks you're a vampire?" said Wilmot. "That's crazy."

"Careful, little dude. You're talking about the girl I love."

"But…" Wilmot realized he didn't know what to say. He shut his mouth. They sat around in silence for what seemed like a long time. When he couldn't take it anymore, Wilmot said softly, "I thought of some new words for the 'Rock Anthem to Principal Hale.'"

"Sorry, little dude," Headcase mumbled from behind his hands. "My music career is finished."

"What?" Wilmot glanced wildly at Wang and Magnolia. "You can't give up on music! We've got a concert coming up!"

"Go on without me, little dudes." Headcase shook his head. "I'll be walking all alone on that Boulevard of Broken Dreams."

"But we need you!" Wilmot protested.

"Sorry, little dude."

"But the show must go on!" Magnolia cried.

"It can go on without me," said Headcase.

"Please," said Wilmot. "Please."

It was no use. Headcase wouldn't change his mind. Finally, they left, the door sighing shut behind them.

Clouds darkened the sky. A biting wind whipped through the street. Flakes of snow whirled in the air. Wilmot hunched his shoulders and shoved his hands deep into his jacket pockets.

"We can do the show without him," Magnolia said as they walked away from the dilapidated house.

"I can't," said Wilmot. "I don't know all the riffs. I need more practice."

"We can practice together," said Wang. "The Dunces never fail!"

Wilmot hunched himself further against the wind. He didn't want to give up. He didn't want to say it was impossible. But he could feel his gut clenching and that old, familiar feeling of despair rising from the pit of his stomach.

"Don't worry, it'll all work out." Wang slapped him on the back as they split up at the corner, each heading their own way home. But walking down the lonely street toward his house, Wilmot couldn't help worrying. Instead of music, his head was filled with thoughts of disaster. He could feel his palms breaking into a sweat. Disconsolate, he dragged his feet up the stairs to his front porch. Guitar in hand, he walked straight in through the front door.

FOURTEEN

Busted

His father was coming down the staircase. Wilmot froze as he caught sight of him: black beard, sharp black eyes, somber brown jacket and tie. For a panicked second, Wilmot thought of ditching the guitar in the coat closet and making a dash for his bedroom. Too late. His father reached the bottom stair and stood directly in front of him.

"What's this?" His father's hand swooped down and plucked the instrument from Wilmot's hands. "A guitar? An *electric* guitar?"

Clenched in his father's grip, the guitar blazed forth proudly—captured, yet unconquered. Its black paint gleamed. Its red thunderbolts flared. The sight jolted Wilmot into courageous action.

"Give it back!" He lunged at the guitar. His fingers raked the metal strings, sending a discordant cry into the air. His father yanked the instrument up, out of Wilmot's reach.

"Is this what you've been doing with your time, Wilmot? Coming home late? Neglecting your studies?"

"But Dad—"

"You told me you were practicing chess with your friends from the club."

"Dad, I—"

"I trusted you, Wilmot. I let you come home late. I thought it was good for you to spend some time with boys your own age. Serious-minded boys. But this?" He shook the guitar. "*This?*"

Wilmot's mother stepped into the hallway. Warm, fragrant air wafted from the kitchen behind her.

"What's going on?" She glanced from Wilmot to his father.

"This!" His father thrust the guitar in her face like a piece of evidence in a horrible crime. "This is how he's been frittering away his time!"

His mother took a step back.

"It's only a musical instrument," she said.

"A musical instrument? You call this a musical instrument?" His father's face had gone red. "If Wilmot wants to play an instrument, he can choose one with some tradition. Some history. Some musical integrity. *This...* why *this* is nothing more than a...a...noisemaker!"

He shook the guitar again, fist clenched around its neck.

"Don't break it, Dad," Wilmot pleaded. "It was a gift."

"A gift?" Mom said.

"A guy gave it to me," said Wilmot. "If I could just show you how I can play..."

"Not under my roof, you won't!" His father brushed past Wilmot, yanked on his winter boots and whipped his long black coat out of the closet.

"Where are you going?" Wilmot cried.

"I'm donating it to the Salvation Army." His father opened the door, letting in a blast of biting-cold air. "I'm sorry, Wilmot. But this so-called instrument is leading you down the wrong path."

He went out, slamming the door behind him.

Wilmot ran to the door. His mother grabbed his arm, but he shook her off. The wind whipped snow into his face as ran onto the front porch. His father was already in the car. Bounding down the walkway, Wilmot grasped the ice-cold handle of the passenger door.

The door was locked. Inside, he saw his father's grim face and the dark shape of the guitar lying on the backseat. He banged on the window. His father revved the engine. Wilmot jumped back. The car roared backward out of the driveway and sped away into the whirling snow and the gathering darkness. Wilmot felt as though his heart had been torn to shreds.

An arm came to rest around his shoulders.

His mom. She stood beside him in the snow, with no coat and only slippers on her feet.

"I need my guitar back, Mom," he pleaded.

"Your father may have a point, Wilmot," she said. "He's a very intelligent man, you know."

"I don't care if he's the smartest guy on earth!"

"He's only trying to do what's best."

"It's not best!" Wilmot sobbed. "It's worst!"

"He's your father, Wilmot," said his mom.

He tore himself away from her, ran upstairs and snatched the phone from his father's study. His father had failed him. His mother had failed him. There was only one thing to do.

Call the Dunces.

The half-hour walk to Magnolia's house left Wilmot shaking—though whether it was from anger, or cold or the fact that he hadn't eaten since lunchtime, he didn't know or care. All he knew was that it wasn't fair, what his father had done.

"He stole my guitar! He stole it!" Wilmot exploded to Josh as he shook off his boots and coat in Magnolia's front hall.

"Calm down, Wil," said Josh. "We'll get it back."

Josh looked awful. His eye was swollen shut, surrounded by a black bruise beneath a purple lump on his forehead. Knowing that it was his fault Josh had joined the hockey team made Wilmot feel even worse. Miserable, Wilmot followed his friend into the dining room.

Wang and Magnolia were sitting at the huge antique dinner table, with Magnolia's baby brother, Garland, in a goober-stained high chair beside them. Magnolia was bribing Garland into eating his carrots with a bag of chocolate-chip cookies—one little bite of carrots…one BIG bite of cookie…one little bite of carrots…one BIG bite of cookie…

Wilmot fell into a chair.

"I need a cookie," he said.

"Take five," said Wang sympathetically. He grabbed a handful of cookies from the bag and piled them on the table in front of Wilmot.

"Thanks," said Wilmot. He ate a cookie. It didn't help.

"My guitar!" he moaned. "I have to get my guitar back!"

"Don't worry," said Magnolia. "I've already thought of a plan."

Magnolia shoved the remainder of a cookie into Garland's mouth and rose slowly from her chair.

"Nocturnia, Vampire Princess of Doom, appears in your father's bedchamber at the last stroke of midnight! In a harrowing voice, she warns, 'Return the guitar to Wilmot, or face the wrath of the Eternally Undead!'"

Wilmot stared at Magnolia. Her hands were raised in a haunting gesture. Her purple velour top was spattered with Garland's carrot spit-up.

He looked at Wang. Wang shrugged.

Garland reached his pudgy fists toward the cookie bag. "Tookie! Tookie!" Crumbs spewed from his half-full mouth.

Magnolia ignored him. "So, guys, great plan, huh?" she said.

"It's not gonna work, Magnolia." Wilmot shook his head. "It's not gonna work in a million years."

"Why not?"

"My dad doesn't believe in vampires."

"Sheesh! What is wrong with people? Don't they have any imagination?"

"Dad says imagination is a modern excuse for daydreaming," said Wilmot. Daydreaming was a waste of time, and time was supposed to be spent wisely, not wasted on useless things. Useless things—like learning to play the guitar.

"Don't worry, Wil," said Josh. "I've got another idea. We'll just go to the Salvation Army store and buy your guitar back. I have some allowance saved up, and I brought it with me. You can keep the guitar at my place. That way, your dad won't have to know."

"Seriously, Josh?" Wilmot looked at Josh's black eye and felt another pang of guilt. "You're always doing stuff for me."

"That's 'cause he's the prez," said Wang.

"It's 'cause you're my friend," said Josh.

"I'll pay you back," said Wilmot. "I'll probably get some money for my birthday."

"That's okay." Josh shrugged. "Whenever."

"Well, what are we waiting for?" Wang jumped from his chair. "Let's get going!"

"Hang on a minute," said Magnolia. "What about Garland? I'm supposed to be babysitting, you know. I can't just leave him here."

She gestured toward her baby brother, who had managed to capture the cookie bag and was busy shoving cookies in his mouth.

"Bring him with us," said Wang.

"I can't bring him." Magnolia crossed her arms. "He's just a baby."

"I not baby!" Garland shouted through a mouth full of crumbs. "I big boy."

"See?" said Wang. "He's a big boy."

"He's a baby," said Magnolia.

"I not baby!" Garland threw a cookie at her.

"Okay, fine," said Magnolia. "I'll bring him. But you guys have to help."

She lifted Garland, still clutching the cookie bag, out of the high chair. Chocolate-chip crumbs and bits of half-chewed carrot showered from his bib onto the floor. Magnolia wiped his face with a dishtowel and put him down.

"Someone has to help me get him into his snow-suit," she said.

"I'll help," said Wang. "Come here, buddy."

He held out his arms and Garland went toddling toward him, a huge smile on his face.

"Ready for your snowsuit, buddy?" Wang said.

"No snow-soo," said Garland, clutching his diaper. "Wang change poopy!"

"Poopy?" Wang made a face.

"The change table's upstairs, in the bathroom," said Magnolia. "Don't look at me. You got yourself into this."

FIFTEEN

I Not Baby

Darkness had fallen by the time they arrived at the Salvation Army Thrift Store. Magnolia gripped the handles of Garland's stroller, fingers cold in her thin, black gloves, head bowed against the bitter wind. Her sense of style had prevented her from wearing the puffy, electric-blue ski mittens her dad had gotten her for Christmas, but that vanity seemed foolish now.

Garland sat in his stroller, muffled from head to toe in warm winter clothes. Only his eyes and nose peeked out from the tiny gap between his woolen tuque and his fuzzy scarf. His nose was a problem though—bright red and oozing a constant stream of mucus. When Magnolia left it uncovered, it froze. When she covered it up, the scarf became encrusted with half-congealed snot.

She realized now that she shouldn't have let the boys talk her into bringing Garland out on a night like this. But it was too late. She could only hope that they'd find the guitar quickly, buy it and get back home before her parents returned. It seemed like a straight-forward plan. At least Garland had a clean diaper on. And he wasn't crying.

The picture window of the Salvation Army Thrift Store looked like a badly organized theater props department. It was filled with old-fashioned tele-phones, mismatched furniture, fancy silverware in faded velvet boxes, two beige filing cabinets and a mannequin wearing a wedding dress with a red-and-white Santa Claus hat on her head. They walked along beside the window until they came to an alcove that led to the entrance door. Magnolia pushed Garland into the shelter of the alcove. Josh yanked on the door handle.

It was locked.

"They're closed," he said.

"Closed!" wailed Wilmot. "How can they be closed? It's only seven thirty!"

"They closed at five o'clock," said Josh, reading a sign on the door.

"Maybe your dad took the guitar back home," said Wang. "The store must have already been closed when he got here."

Wilmot said nothing but pressed his face against the glass door, trying to locate his guitar among the dimly lit shelves of ugly dishware.

"I bet he left it in there." Magnolia pointed to the donation drop box beside the door.

The drop box looked like a huge mailbox. It had a large metal door that opened downward, with a metal handle and a sign that said *After Hours Donations*. Magnolia tugged on the handle.

"Is it there?" said Wilmot.

Magnolia tried to peer into the drop box, but it was no use. Like on a mailbox, the metal door of the drop box opened to form a V-shaped compartment. The back wall of the V tilted up to block the opening, making it impossible to see inside the drop box. Obviously, people were meant to put their donations into the compartment and close the door. Then the compartment would tip to the inside, dumping the donations into the box. It was just like mailing a package.

"Someone's got to go in there!" cried Wang. He whipped an Amazing Spiderman flashlight out of his jacket pocket. "Have no fear! Wang is here!"

"Are you crazy?" said Magnolia.

"Give me a boost!" Wang answered. He opened the drop-box door, lifted one leg into the metal compartment, grabbed Magnolia's shoulders for support and swung his second leg in.

"You're not going to fit," Magnolia groaned, as the weight of Wang's body pressed down on her shoulders.

"Observe the Amazing Pretzel Man!" Wang exclaimed. He scrunched his knees and curled his head to his chest, lying in the compartment like a baby in a cradle.

"You're bum's sticking out!" warned Josh.

"The Amazing Pretzel Man can fit into the smallest crevice!" came Wang's muffled reply. "Close the door!"

Magnolia began to ease the metal door closed. But the weight of Wang's body made the compartment tip too quickly, and she could barely keep hold of the handle as the door slammed with a crunch onto Wang's protruding buttocks.

"OWWWWWWWW!" Wang howled. "Abort mission! Abort mission!"

Josh grabbed hold of the handle. He and Magnolia ripped the door open. Wang tumbled out and fell to the ground.

"Ow! Ow!" he cried, grabbing his rear end. "Ow, my aching butt!"

"This is crazy," said Magnolia. "Why don't we come back tomorrow after school? I bet the guitar will still be there."

"Good idea," said Josh.

But Wilmot jumped forward.

"No way!" he exclaimed. "I'm going in."

Magnolia looked at Wilmot skeptically. The kid had lost his mind. Although he was smaller than Wang, he was also much less athletic. He wasn't exactly fat— not even chubby, really. He was just short and kind of soft. Like a gummy bear. And while it was possible to imagine Wang pulling off the daring guitar rescue in the guise of the Amazing Pretzel Man, this was not a mission that could be entrusted to a gummy bear.

But Wilmot was already trying to lift one stocky leg into the donation box.

"Give me a hand, Josh," he said.

Josh bent down and interlaced his hands to make a step. Wilmot put one foot in the step, grabbed the top of Josh's head and hoisted the other foot into the metal compartment.

"Push me in! Push me in!" he shouted. Josh tried to lift up Wilmot's second leg and shove it into the compartment. But no one was holding the handle, and the door began to tilt closed, yanking Wilmot's legs apart in the Russian splits.

Gummy bears were not built for the Russian splits.

"Help! Help! Abort mission! Abort mission!" Wilmot screamed.

Magnolia sprang forward and yanked on the handle. Wilmot lunged to escape. His body collided with Josh's head. Josh hit the pavement. Wilmot sprawled on top of him.

"Ow! My groin! My aching groin!" cried Wilmot.

"Ow! My head! My aching head!" moaned Josh.

Magnolia looked down at the heap of boys at her feet.

"This is ridiculous," she said. "I'm going home. No one's going to fit into that thing."

"Wait!" cried Wang. "There is *one* person who would fit."

He looked at Garland in his stroller.

Garland stared back, wide-eyed.

"No way." Magnolia stepped in front of the stroller. "He's not going in there. He's only a baby."

"I not baby!" His wooly scarf couldn't muffle the insulted tone in Garland's voice. "I big boy!"

"See?" said Wang. "He's a big boy."

"He's a baby."

"I not baby! I NOT baby! I NOT BABY!" Garland screamed.

Great. Now they'd set him off. Magnolia crouched beside the stroller to calm him down, but it was no use. Garland was in full temper-tantrum mode. His legs flailed. His boots went flying. One of them hit Wilmot in the head.

"Ow! My brain! My aching brain!" moaned Wilmot.

His feeble complaint was no match for Garland.

"I BIG BOY!" he screamed. "NO WANT STROLLER!"

Garland bucked against the straps that held him in the baby stroller. He flung his mittens on the ground. He tore off his hat and scarf.

"Garland! Stop it!" shouted Magnolia. What if an adult came along and found them like this? They were all going to get in big trouble. Her parents would be home soon too. What if she wasn't there? Garland was supposed to be in bed, not out chasing after Wilmot's guitar. This mission was over. She and Garland were going home.

She stooped to pick up Garland's boots and mittens from the sidewalk. But when she straightened and turned to put them back on, Garland wasn't in his stroller. She looked around frantically. Had he escaped? No, he was huddled in Wang's arms, clinging to his neck as though Wang were the only person in the whole wide world who understood his sorrows.

"You're a big boy, right, Garland?" said Wang.

Garland nodded, tears in his eyes.

"You want to go on a mission, right, Garland?" said Wang.

Garland nodded.

"He doesn't even know what a mission is!" Magnolia stamped her foot. This was getting ridiculous.

"You want to save the guitar, right?" said Wang.

Garland nodded.

"He doesn't even know what a guitar is!"

"Wiggle! Wiggle!" said Garland.

The Wiggles were his favorite kiddy band.

"Okay, fine, he knows what a guitar is! But he can't go on a mission. This is crazy."

"You can take my Amazing Spiderman flashlight," said Wang.

Garland's eyes opened wide. He grabbed the flashlight in his pudgy, mitten-less hands.

"You can't do this," said Magnolia.

Wang carried Garland to the donation box, opened the compartment door and gently placed him inside.

"You go in there. You find the guitar. You climb back in here. And we bring you back out. Okay?" said Wang.

Garland nodded. He clutched the flashlight to his chest. The beam lit up his wide, innocent eyes.

"This is not a good idea," said Magnolia.

"Please, Magnolia!" Wilmot came up beside her. "I really need my guitar. Garland's our only hope."

"He can do it. He's a big boy. Right, buddy?" said Wang.

Garland nodded.

Slowly, Wang began to tilt the metal door closed. The gap through which Magnolia could see her baby brother's face grew smaller and smaller. As it did, Garland's eyes grew wider and wider until, at the last millisecond, they suddenly filled with panic.

"I not big boy!" Garland cried in a piteous voice. "I baaaa-beee!"

Clunk!

The door slammed shut.

"Get him out of there! Get him out!" Magnolia screamed.

She pushed Wang aside, grabbed the cold metal handle and yanked the door open.

Dunces Rock

It was too late.

Garland had disappeared inside the drop box. And from the dark depths of that metal dungeon came a heart-wrenching cry.

"Maaaaa-maaaaa!"

SIXTEEN

Rescuing Garland

"I'm going in," said Wang.

"You can't!" Magnolia turned on him. "You're too big! This is all your fault!"

"I'll rescue Garland if it's the last thing I do!" Wang vowed.

On the ground below them, Josh was on his hands and knees.

"Hold still, Prez!" Wang climbed onto Josh's back as though it were a step stool.

"Oof!" said Josh.

"Don't move!" said Wang.

"You're still not gonna fit," said Magnolia.

"I'm going in headfirst!" Wang announced. "Close it halfway and I'll slither through."

"It's not gonna work."

"It might work," said Wilmot.

"Maaaa-maaaa!" cried Garland from inside the drop box.

Wang wedged his head and torso into the metal compartment. He lifted his feet off of Josh's back and wriggled himself inside, until only his legs stuck out.

"Now! Tilt it!" Wang called. His voice sounded like it came from inside a metal pail.

"You're gonna get stuck!" said Magnolia.

"No, I'm not!"

"Waaaaaaah!" cried Garland.

"Give me a push!" shouted Wang.

Magnolia and Josh each grabbed one of Wang's boots and began pushing. Wilmot hung on to the handle. Baby Garland wailed from inside the drop box.

Then a hand landed on Magnolia's shoulder, and the deep, heavy voice of an adult said, "Do you kids mind telling me what you're doing?"

Magnolia whipped around, yanking Wang's foot with her. Wang came flailing out of the drop box and collapsed on the ground.

Magnolia raised her head. An adult's face looked down at her. A face beneath a policeman's cap.

"Yes?" said the officer.

"My baby brother!" blurted Magnolia. "He's stuck inside there!"

The police officer stepped forward. He unhooked a flashlight from his belt and opened the door to the drop box. He shone his flashlight in, but the back of the metal compartment blocked the beam. Garland's voice wafted up from the depths. "Maaaa-maaaa!"

"How long has he been in there?" demanded the policeman, turning to Magnolia.

"I don't know," Magnolia answered. She felt a mixture of dread and relief at the arrival of the Force of the Law.

"I'll call the Salvation Army. Someone must have a key."

The policeman strode to his car, opened the door and pulled out a CB radio. Magnolia huddled with the three boys in the alcove, listening to Garland's muffled cries. She couldn't stand it anymore. She opened the drop-box door.

"It's okay, Garland. You're going to be out soon," she called down.

"Nolia!" Garland cried.

Magnolia shivered. Her jeans were soaked through. Her hands felt numb.

The policeman finished the call on the radio and came back to them.

"They're on their way." He stared down at Magnolia. "How old is your little brother, Miss?"

"He's only two!"

"Only two? How did he get in there?"

Magnolia sniffled. She looked around at the boys. It was all Wang's fault. He should have known better than to shove a baby down the donation chute like a pair of secondhand sneakers. But when she looked at Wang's face, she knew she couldn't rat him out. How could she betray the Amazing Pretzel Man? Besides, he was only trying to help Wilmot. And Wilmot looked so miserable that she couldn't tell on him either.

She looked at Josh. He seemed as though he was counting on her to come up with some dramatic story, like the act that had won the heart of Principal Hale. But telling a story to Principal Hale was one thing. Telling a story to a policeman? That was probably a crime. She could probably be thrown in jail for dramatification of justice.

She looked up at the policeman and immediately looked down again.

"I'm not sure, sir," she mumbled. "I just turned my back on him, and I guess he climbed in."

"Your baby brother climbed in? All by himself?"

"I guess so."

"All by himself?"

The police officer gave her a steely look.

"I didn't really see," Magnolia mumbled.

"What about you boys?" He turned to Wang, Wilmot and Josh. "Did you see anything?"

Wilmot shrugged. Wang shook his head. Josh kept his mouth shut.

"Well then, Miss," said the officer, turning back to Magnolia. "You'd better give me your parents' phone number. Either that or you'll all have to come down to the station."

"The police station?" said Magnolia.

"Are we going to get fingerprinted?" said Wang. "Cool!"

Magnolia elbowed him in the ribs.

"Sorry," muttered Wang. "But it would be cool."

"Are we going to jail?" wailed Wilmot.

"I think I can let your parents deal with it—this time." The officer frowned. "But I'm going to need that phone number."

Magnolia hung her head.

"Okay."

The police officer pulled a notepad out of his breast pocket, and Magnolia gave him her dad's cell number. A few minutes later, she and the boys were sitting in the warm backseat of the police car while the officer stood guard outside the drop box, waiting for her parents and the Salvation Army people to arrive.

An uncomfortable silence filled the back of the police car. Magnolia didn't feel like looking at the boys, let alone talking to them. Didn't they know the difference between a cunning plan and an idiotic shenanigan?

"I am going to get into so much trouble for this," she finally said.

"Please don't tell on me, Magnolia," Wilmot pleaded. "My dad, he'll probably send me to reform school or something."

"I'm not going to tell on you! Sheesh! What do you think I am, a tattletale?"

"It's my fault, Magnolia," said Wang. "I'm sorry."

"You were only trying to get my guitar," Wilmot said. "And besides, you tried to rescue Garland."

"Yeah, after you dumped him in the donation box," said Magnolia. "Sheesh! My mom is going to freak."

"It'll all work out," whispered Josh. He didn't sound too certain.

A van pulled up behind them and stopped at the curb. The headlights shone through the back window of the police car, bathing everything in a weird, white light. A woman got out of the van and hurried toward the drop box, a big purse slung over her shoulder and a set of keys in her hand. She crouched down in front of the box. A few seconds later, a big metal door swung open and piles of clothes tumbled out, mixed with cardboard boxes, plastic bags and old books. Climbing over the heap on pudgy legs came Garland. He was holding something in his hands—something as big as he was, with a long, narrow neck and an arrow-shaped body.

"My guitar!" cried Wilmot.

"He did it!" exclaimed Wang. "Way to go, Garland!"

"I don't believe it," muttered Magnolia, yet she couldn't help feeling proud of her little brother.

Another set of headlights shone through the windows, and Magnolia's parents' van pulled up and parked at the curb in front of the police car. The taillights hadn't even shut off when the passenger-side door swung open and Magnolia's mother bounded out of the van and swept Garland into her arms. Magnolia's father got out of the driver's side and walked over to the police officer and the Salvation

Army lady, who was shoving the pile of secondhand stuff back into the drop box.

Snow fell in tiny flakes, casting a haze over the scene, lit only by the headlamps of the Salvation Army van and the glow of the lights in the thrift-store display window. Magnolia could see her dad talking to the Salvation Army lady. He gestured toward Garland, still holding the guitar as he pressed himself tightly against the furry collar of his mother's coat. The lady picked up a teddy bear from the heap of stuff and approached. She held it out to Garland.

"What's she doing?" said Magnolia.

Wang, Josh and Wilmot leaned over her, craning to see through the window.

"She's giving him a teddy bear," said Wang.

"No," said Josh. "Look! She's holding out her hand. She wants to make a trade."

"A trade?" gasped Wilmot. "She wants him to trade my guitar for a teddy bear? No! Don't do it, Garland!"

"Remember your mission!" cried Wang.

The lady stepped closer to Garland, waving the teddy bear in his face.

Garland shook his head.

"Atta boy!" said Wilmot.

"He'll never surrender!" said Wang.

The lady made the teddy bear dance up and down. Garland shook his head. The lady reached into her purse and took something out. Magnolia pressed her face against the window.

Oh, no. Not that.

"Cookies!" she gasped.

"Not cookies!" Wilmot moaned.

"She's discovered his weakness!" exclaimed Wang.

The lady held out a cookie to Garland. He hesitated. She waved the cookie up and down. He reached for it. She slipped the guitar from his weakened grasp.

"Noooooo!" cried Wilmot. He launched himself across Magnolia's lap and yanked at the door handle. The door didn't budge.

"We're locked in!" he cried.

"Of course we're locked in." Magnolia bucked him off her lap. "You don't think they let criminals escape from the back of cop cars, do you?"

"But I'm not a criminal! That's my guitar! Mine!" Wilmot clawed at the window. The lady turned away and placed the guitar on top of the heap of junk inside the drop box. She closed the door and locked it.

"So close!" Wilmot slumped against the back of the seat and sunk his head in his hands. "So close!"

A few moments later, the door of the police car opened with a blast of cold air.

"Out you get, kids," said Magnolia's dad. "Come on. I'll drive you home."

Magnolia put her arm around Wilmot and guided him onto the sidewalk.

"It's all right, Wilmot," she said. "You tried your best."

They filed into Magnolia's minivan, silent, heads hung down. Magnolia's mom was sitting in the backseat, clutching Garland and crying, "Oh my baby, my baby."

Garland had cookie crumbs all over his cheeks.

"Good try, buddy," Wang whispered as he sat down beside him. "It wasn't your fault."

They buckled their seat belts and Magnolia's dad put the van in motion. Slowly they drove down the dark streets. All was silent except for her mom's cooing.

Finally, Wang spoke up. "It was my fault, sir. Not Magnolia's."

"I'm sure there's enough blame to go around," Magnolia's dad said, his voice tight and angry.

No one spoke again for a few blocks, until they stopped at a stop sign and Magnolia's father turned around to face them.

"I'm sure you all had your parts to play in this. But Magnolia was the one entrusted with keeping her baby brother safe. She was the babysitter. She should have known better."

"I'm sorry," said Magnolia. She hung her head.

"Sorry's not good enough this time, Magnolia," her father said. "From now on, no more going out on weekends. No more visiting friends after school. No clubs. No activities. No talking on the phone. No texting. No TV. No computer games. For one month, young lady, you are grounded."

SEVENTEEN

The Lion's Choice

A buzz of anticipation electrified the air in the community center's fitness room on Saturday morning, and despite feeling sorry for his friends' troubles, Wang couldn't help the tingle of excitement that ran down his spine and sent his toes jittering. Today Master Hui Bing would finally choose the two best dancers in the class to perform the lion dance at the upcoming talent show—one to play the head of the lion, and one to play the tail.

For the audition, each dancer had to perform an original, two-minute routine. Wang had practiced his routine every evening for weeks. He knew it so well he could have danced it in his sleep. He could have danced it even if an evil sorcerer tried to wipe it out of his brain with a mind-altering spell. He knew the steps of the lion backward and forward, up, down and sideways. But the wisdom of the lion? He had to admit, he was worried about the wisdom.

Wang had listened carefully to Master Hui Bing's words in class, but they still made no sense to him. He did not know the heart of the lonely rutabaga. *Face it*, he told himself as he looked around the room at the mass of kids preparing to compete for the two precious spots. *You're not wise.* After all, a wise man wouldn't have shoved a two-year-old down the Salvation Army Thrift Store donation-box chute. A wise man would have picked the lock. Or sawed through it. Or dynamited it. Well, maybe not dynamited it. But he would have done something. Also, a wise man would have figured out a way to save the Drama and Music program. Wang wasn't a wise man. He was just a Dunce.

Still, he was a Dunce with some great dance moves. After many attempts and a few bruised ribs, he had finally mastered the trick of running up the wall and flipping over backward. This was the centerpiece of the dance routine he intended to perform to convince Master Hui Bing of his worthiness to play the lion.

Wang spotted Josh coming through the door of the fitness room and waved him over.

"You ready?" said Wang as Josh sat on the floor beside him.

"I'm not gonna try out. Are you kidding?" Josh pointed to his black eye.

"You could still give it a shot."

"Naw. I just came to keep you company."

Wang looked around the room, scoping out the competition. Despite what Josh had told him about the brothers Shawn and Al Tung, Wang couldn't take them seriously as dancers. They could barely unicorn-step without tripping over their own feet. He figured his main competition would come from Zahraa, who'd combined break dancing and lion dancing into a style all her own.

When the hands on the clock marked exactly 8:00 AM, Master Hui Bing strode into the room. As always, Wang felt the power of his presence. A force field of strength and wisdom surrounded him. The kids fell silent and formed themselves into rows. The master bowed. The kids bowed back.

The master shook his wavy, blond mane of hair.

"Today," he said in his sonorous voice, "the lion shall choose."

A large drum stood in the corner of the room. A man the same age as Hui Bing entered and took his stance behind the drum. The master ordered the students to sit in a large circle. He held up his hands for silence.

"The dance of the lion calls for strength and wisdom!" he proclaimed. "Grace is in his steps, and nobility in his heart! A million million grains of sand are in the desert, but what is the grain that sticks beneath my toenail?"

He cast his hypnotic glance around the circle. No one spoke.

"Very well," said the master. "Who dares to dance first?"

Wang shot up his hand and sprang into the center of the circle. "Oh! Oh! I'll go!"

"Very well," said Hui Bing. "Silence for the first dancer!"

Wang crouched low and waited for the drumming to begin. The steps he'd practiced whirled in his head. At the first beat of the drum, he leaped in the air, kicked his legs into the splits and touched his toes. He landed, spun around and threw a cartwheel.

At the front of the room, Master Hui Bing nodded his approval.

To the beat of the drum, Wang began to unicorn-step. First right. Then left. Then around in a circle. The circle grew tighter and tighter. He began to spin, kicking one leg out and turning on the other. Around and around. The drums beat faster. The kids in the circle around him were nothing but a whir of color. His reflection flashed at him from the mirrored walls. At last he stopped spinning. He struck a horse stance. Now for the grand finale. He busted through the circle of kids, took a running leap at the one unmirrored wall, planted his left foot, then his right foot, pushed off of his right leg and flung himself into the air, flipped over backward and landed perfectly. Three final beats marked the end of the drumming. Wang drew himself up straight. He bowed deeply to Master Hui Bing. He turned and bowed to the class as they applauded his performance.

"That was great!" Josh whispered as Wang slid into place beside him in the circle.

"Thanks!" he panted. He felt exhilarated—out of breath, yet at the same time full of energy. He had given his best effort. He could do nothing more but wait for the lion to choose.

Wang sat catching his breath as the other dancers performed their routines one by one. Some were good.

Others—like Shawn and Al Tung—were terrible. Wang only half paid attention to them. He was waiting for Zahraa to perform. At last, she stepped into the center, and the circle grew silent, waiting for the drumming to begin.

From the first beat, Wang knew she would outperform anyone else. One moment she leaped high in the air, the next moment she spun on her head on the floor. It was two minutes of nonstop action, and when she finished her routine, the class erupted into applause.

"That was amazing," Wang said to Josh under his breath.

"You were just as good," Josh whispered back. "Don't worry—you were awesome."

When Zahraa had taken her place in the circle, Master Hui Bing strode to the center.

"You have performed well!" he announced. "Now the lion shall choose!"

Master Hui Bing closed his eyes and raised his hands, inviting the spirit of the lion to come into him and choose the dancers. The drum began to beat, soft and low. Master Hui Bing's bare feet began to move. His eyes remained closed as he started to walk and then dance around the circle, humming and reaching with his hands into the air as though to feel the cosmic energy of the lion. His hair streamed out behind him as he spun and tossed his head. He wavered. He seemed to hesitate in front of Wang, and then he danced on, drawn this time toward Zahraa. He tossed his hair at her, swaying, as the drum beat faster. A loud drumbeat rang out. The lion was about to make his choice. Master Hui Bing leaped in the air. He spun. He landed. He landed in front of Shawn and Al Tung.

"The lion has chosen!" Master Hui Bing announced.

A gasp went around the circle.

"I knew it," Josh muttered, sinking his head in his hands.

"What!" Wang hissed, not daring to raise his voice above a whisper.

Zahraa jumped to her feet.

"That's not fair!" she shouted.

"Do you dare to question the choice of the lion?" Hui Bing thundered.

Zahraa stood her ground for a second. She looked very small and thin compared to the powerful figure of Master Hui Bing. She wavered. She took a step backward. She sat down.

"The lion has spoken!" Hui Bing proclaimed. He stood in the center of the circle, hands on his hips, daring anyone to challenge him. The kids stared at the floor. Wang's heart pounded. He stole a glance at Zahraa. He wished he was brave enough to jump up and defy the master as she had done, but his body felt weak, paralyzed.

Master Hui Bing turned and walked out of the room.

The silence lasted a second longer, and then everyone began talking at once. It was Zahraa who expressed the thought in Wang's mind—Wang himself did not dare to say it out loud.

"That," said Zahraa, "was a load of baloney."

EIGHTEEN

A Cunning Plan

Monday rolled around and Wang still couldn't believe the lion had chosen Shawn and Al. He was a better dancer than they were. He knew it. Zahraa was a better dancer too. It must be true, what Josh had said: Shawn and Al only got the part because their dad had given Master Hui Bing a break on rent. It wasn't the lion that had chosen them, it was Master Hui Bing himself. No, not Master Hui Bing. Larry. It was plain old Larry who had chosen them. And his choice was not noble or fair. His choice stunk. Larry was no Wise Warrior. He was a fake. His sayings were gibberish. There was no beating heart in a rutabaga. The wise man washed his socks in a washing machine, like everyone else.

Losing the lion dance wouldn't have been so bad if Wang could have looked forward to playing drums in Headcase's band at the Principal's Challenge Cup hockey game. But the game was less than three weeks away, and as far as Wang could tell, the band was deader than roadkill.

The day after their failed rescue expedition, they had run to the Salvation Army Thrift Store at lunch hour to buy Wilmot's guitar back. But they'd come too late—the instrument had already been sold. Wilmot had fallen into a silent funk, and with Magnolia already grouchy at being grounded, a deep gloom had descended over Dunces Anonymous. The situation seemed hopeless. Wang didn't say that to Josh, though, when the president suggested holding an emergency lunch-hour meeting at Wang's house that Monday morning. They couldn't meet in their classroom because Stacey Hogarth was holding a meeting of her Spirit Committee, which was plotting to barge in and take over the intermission show.

"I talked to the principal at practice this weekend, and he still wants the band to perform," said Josh as they all grabbed seats at Wang's kitchen table.

"Problem," said Wang. "We don't have a band."

"Problem," added Magnolia. "We don't have a guitarist."

"Problem," moaned Wilmot. "We don't even have a guitar."

"Don't give up, you guys!" said Josh. "All we need is a cunning plan."

"The show must go on," Magnolia agreed halfheartedly.

"Yeah," said Wang. "But how?"

Josh took a sandwich out of his lunch bag. Josh's mom always packed him gourmet sandwiches, because she didn't understand that kids' stomachs do not like adult food. They were made out of bread that looked like tree bark, smeared with something-or-other pâté and topped with leafy green stuff that kind of looked like lettuce and kind of not.

"What's that?" Wang pointed at the lettuce-like thing.

"Mom says it's called arugula." Josh scrunched up his nose.

Arugula. It didn't even sound like a vegetable. It sounded like a place you'd never return from alive. The Evil Isle of Arugula.

"Do you want peanut butter on toast instead?" said Wang.

"Yeah." Josh tossed his sandwich in the kitchen compost.

Wang made toast with peanut butter for Josh and himself. It was weird how peanut butter gummed up your mouth but made your brain work better than ever. Wang might have asked Master Hui Bing about that paradox, if only Hui Bing hadn't turned out to be such a big phony.

"Listen, guys, I have an idea," Josh said, biting into his toast. "We have to go back to when all our problems started. You know, like when you lose something and you try to remember the last time you saw it."

"That'd be when my dad took my guitar away," said Wilmot.

"No. It was before that. When Headcase's girlfriend broke up with him," said Magnolia.

"Yeah," Wang agreed. "That's what started everything. Then Headcase said he wasn't going to play in the band anymore. Then Wil's dad took his guitar away. Then Magnolia got grounded. Then Larry picked Al and Shawn for the lion dance. Everything went wrong. It was like the Curse of the Dumped Boyfriend."

"And now, things will never get better unless we can find some way to undo the curse!" Wilmot exclaimed, and he sunk his head into his hands.

"I know!" said Magnolia. She pushed back her chair and jumped to her feet. "Nocturnia, Vampire Princess of Doom—"

"Not the Vampire Princess of Doom again!" Wilmot groaned.

"Hang on," said Wang. "Give her a chance."

"Thank you, Wang," said Magnolia. She spread her arms dramatically. "As I was saying, Nocturnia, Vampire Princess of Doom, summons the vampire Headcase to appear before her."

"He's not really a vampire," Wilmot mumbled from between his hands.

"Shush!" said Wang.

"The princess is displeased!" Magnolia raised her voice. "Headcase refuses to suck the blood of human beings. He has broken the sacred Vow of the Vampires! Now he must be punished! With a magical spell, she strips away his vampire powers and turns him into a mere, mortal human being!"

"He's already a mere, mortal human being," grumbled Wilmot.

"Wilmot!" said Wang. "Don't you get it? If Headcase gets unvampired, his girlfriend will get back together with him."

"Exactly," said Magnolia. She sat down at the table and bit into her sandwich. "And if his girlfriend gets back together with him, he's happy. And if he's happy, he starts playing music again. Then the band gets back together, and we play our concert at the hockey game, and Principal Hale loves it so much, he brings back the Drama and Music Program."

"Sounds like a cunning plan!" said Wang.

"Exactly," said Josh. "It could work."

"But what about his webbed feet?" Wilmot objected. "How's she going to believe he's not a vampire if he still has webbed feet?"

Magnolia put on her vampire voice.

"Nocturnia, Vampire Princess of Doom, decrees that Headcase's webbed feet must remain forever, as a reminder of the vampire that he once was!"

"But Magnolia," Wilmot argued, "how are you going to do all this stuff? Aren't you supposed to be grounded?"

"Nocturnia, Vampire Princess of Doom, cannot be grounded by mere mortals!"

"I don't think parents count as mere mortals," muttered Wilmot.

"Look, Wilmot." Magnolia picked up Wang's peanut-buttery knife and pointed it at him. "Do you want to get the Drama and Music program back or not?"

"Yeah, but…"

"Well then?"

"But it's not gonna work…"

"Of course it's gonna work. Look, this is what we're going to do. We'll ask Headcase to set up a meeting with Freya. In a park. At, say, eight o'clock at night, this Friday. He can tell her he has some stuff to give back to her, or whatever. Then we jump out of the shrubbery."

"*We?*" said Wilmot.

"Well, I'm not doing this all by myself!"

"Magnolia's right," said Josh. "We're a club. We've got to stick together. Everybody's got to be something. Like, I could be the Vampire Prince of Doom."

Wang tried to picture Josh as the Vampire Prince of Doom. He was kind of short and—although he really liked Josh—kind of runty. And his hair was kind of flat. And besides, his black eye and the big purple bump on his head made him look more like something from a zombie movie. A zombie movie! That was it!

"No, Josh! You should be the zombie slave!"

"Zombie slave? No fair! Why can't I be the vampire prince?"

"But Josh, that lump on your forehead is all purple and green and you've got a really gruesome black eye, and no offense, but…"

"Wang's right—you already look like a zombie. We can't let it.go to waste," Magnolia said.

"Okay, fine." Josh sighed. "I'm the zombie slave."

"Right," said Magnolia. "What about you, Wil?"

"Nothing," Wilmot mumbled, head still sunk on the table.

"You can't be nothing."

"I'm nothing," mumbled Wilmot.

"You're not nothing!"

"I could be a musician. If I had my guitar…" His voice trailed off.

"It's okay, Wil." Josh put an arm around his shoulders. "What about you, Wang? Do you want to be the Vampire Prince of Doom?"

Vampire Prince of Doom sounded pretty cool. He could wear fangs and a long cape. On the other hand, that would mean he was married to Magnolia, which would be weird. And icky. There had to be some other role, some other idea he could come up with. He could almost hear an idea whispering to him in the corner of his brain, in a voice so soft he couldn't quite make out the words.

"Shhh." Wang held up a hand.

"We didn't say anything," said Josh.

"You're crunching your toast."

Josh stopped crunching. The kitchen fell silent. Wang heard the voice in his head—a rough-edged, growling voice.

The lion shall dance for a noble cause. The dancer shall know when he is chosen.

The lion! Of course! It was still in the basement storage room! Larry had betrayed it by picking the wrong dancers, and now the lion was speaking to him, choosing him! What cause could be nobler than bringing Drama and Music back to their school?

Wang drew himself up tall.

"I," he said, "shall be the lion."

NINETEEN

The Clan Balcanquall

It was hopeless, Wilmot thought as he shambled home from school that afternoon. The vampire princess, the zombie slave, the dancing lion—it was all a crazy scheme. It would never work, not in a million years. Worst of all, he knew his friends were only trying to help him. And helping him had already caused them so much trouble.

If not for Wilmot, Josh would never have joined the hockey team. He wouldn't have gotten a huge bump on his head. Magnolia wouldn't have been grounded for trying to rescue the electric guitar. Wang wouldn't have lost the lion dance to Shawn and Al Tung—well, that probably wasn't true, but somehow Wilmot felt responsible for it anyway. *I bring bad luck to everyone*, he thought.

Passing by Headcase's house, Wilmot gazed at the tiny, dark basement windows. He remembered the first time he'd seen the guitar, there on the curb at the end of the driveway. If only he could hold it one more time! If only he could play one more jam session in Headcase's basement! But those days were gone forever. Buying a new electric guitar would cost more money than Wilmot had—even if he could manage to keep the instrument a secret from his dad.

Wilmot dragged his weary feet up the steps to his front porch and opened the front door. His father was waiting for him in the hallway. He probably had a list of mathematical equations for Wilmot to solve before supper. Oh well. It wasn't as though he had anything else to do. He dumped his backpack on the floor. He barely noticed that his father was wearing a skirt.

"Wilmot," his father said. "I've been waiting for you."

Wilmot didn't say anything. He wasn't really speaking to his dad these days.

"Listen to me, Wilmot," his father continued. "I know you're unhappy about the loss of your... instrument...the other day. But I have something to show you. Something important."

Wilmot looked up. His dad was behaving very strangely. Not only did he have a weird gleam in his eye, but—now that Wilmot thought about it—it was very odd that he was wearing a skirt. The skirt, which hung down to just above his dad's knees, was patterned in a red-and-green plaid. He was also wearing a white dress shirt, a plaid tie, a silly red pom-pom cap and a pair of white socks with plaid bands and red tassels. His knees poked out from the top of the socks. They were knobby and round and covered in black hair.

"You've got hairy knees, Dad," Wilmot said.

"Someday, when you are a man, your knees will be hairy too, son!" his father answered. "It is the mark of the men of the Balcanquall clan! You will wear the Balcanquall tartan with pride!"

His father turned on one heel and strode into the living room.

"The Barnacle clan?" Wilmot muttered, trailing after him. It sounded like the crew of a lame pirate movie.

"Not Barnacle, Balcanquall!" His father raised a finger in the air. "Before our name was changed to Binkle by uneducated immigration officers, your ancestors bore the proud Scottish surname of Balcanquall."

Balcanquall? Scottish ancestors? Wilmot didn't even know he *had* Scottish ancestors. Besides, weren't all Scottish people called *Mc*Something? Like McDougall and McAllister and McLean and McDonald? Wouldn't that make him a McBarnacle? McBarnacle sounded like a seafood dish in a lame fast-food restaurant.

"Yes, Balcanquall!" his father continued. "And this, my son, is the Balcanquall family heirloom that has been passed down from generation to generation."

His father swept his hand toward a dark wooden box that sat on the living-room carpet. It looked like an old-fashioned toolbox. Its lid was fastened with brass hinges. It had a brass handle on top and brass hooks to hold it closed. The wood was scratched and dented, but it shone as though it had been recently polished, and the brass fittings gleamed. His father stroked the box.

"Nearly two centuries ago," he began, "your great-great-great-grandfather, Angus Balcanquall, was driven from Scotland by famine and political strife. He was a lad of only sixteen when he set off on a perilous voyage to seek his fortune in the New World. He left home with nothing but the clothes on his back and *this* musical instrument in his hand."

A musical instrument? Wilmot stared at the mysterious box. It was too small to hold a guitar. Maybe a banjo? Or a ukulele? Maybe a flute. Or a clarinet.

Maybe a saxophone. Were saxophones even invented in the olden days of Angus Balcanquall?

"For four generations," his father continued, "this instrument has been passed down from father to son. I played it too, when I was young. But as I pursued my mathematical studies, I felt that I needed silence to concentrate. I felt that every moment I spent on music was a moment stolen from more serious endeavors. The less I practiced, the less I was able to play. Perhaps I never had the musical gift that would have done justice to this instrument. At last, I put it away. Before this afternoon, I hadn't touched it in years. But now, Wilmot, the time has come for the musical legacy of the Balcanqualls to rise again!"

Dad opened the brass hooks and raised the wooden lid. A smell of bacon grease and leather wafted into the air. Gently, his father lifted something out of the box. Something—but what was it? It looked like a dead animal with a limp brown body, a long snout and spindly legs.

"What is it?" Wilmot asked.

"These, my son, are the noble bagpipes."

His father stuck one of the spindly things in his mouth. He puffed on it until the limp body inflated into an oval-shaped leather bag. He tucked the bag under his arm. Three other spindly things—the pipes, Wilmot now realized—rose from the bag and rested against his father's shoulder. They were made of dark wood, fitted with ivory and silver knobs and decorated with tassels that matched the tassels on his father's socks. One last spindly thing stuck out of the bottom of the bag, and Wilmot noticed that it had holes in it, like a flute. His father grasped it, fit his fingers over the holes and marched toward the front door. His skirt—which Wilmot now recognized as a kilt—flapped around his hairy knees. Wilmot wondered which underwear his dad wore beneath the kilt. Hopefully, not the yellow ones with the pink smiley faces, which Wilmot's mother had gotten him for Christmas.

"Where are you going, Dad?"

"The pipes must breathe! The pipes must have air! The pipes yearn for the great open spaces!" his dad cried.

He's gone nuts, Wilmot thought.

Wilmot's dad shoved on his boots and flung open the front door.

"It's snowing!" Wilmot said.

"I shall now play 'Over the Lochs Blooms the Bonny, Bonny Phlox,'" his dad announced. He stepped onto the front porch and took a deep breath.

All was peaceful in the quiet street. Shimmering flakes of snow drifted down from the soft, gray clouds. Tiny white lights twinkled in the pine tree in old Mrs. Twindlethorpe's yard, while old Mrs. Twindlethorpe herself gently swept the snow off her doorstep with a straw broom. Farther down the street, a dog snoozed on his porch, nose tucked into his tail. It was an idyllic winter scene.

Wilmot's father blew on the bagpipes.

An earsplitting screech tore the air. Mrs. Twindlethorpe dropped her broom and slammed her hands over her ears. The dog rocketed to its feet, barking.

Wilmot's father began to march. Knees raised high, he marched down the steps and onto the sidewalk, stepping in time with the discordant keening of the pipes. It sounded like the piercing, off-key wail of a malfunctioning police siren.

"Stop that infernal racket!" Mrs. Twindlethorpe shouted. Wilmot's father marched down the sidewalk toward her. Neighbors stuck their heads out of doors and windows. Wilmot wondered if he should run after his father and bring him home. But there seemed no way of stopping him.

Old Mrs. Twindlethorpe grabbed her broom from the front stoop and ran down her walkway.

"Stop that caterwauling or I'll bean you over the head!" she shouted.

Wilmot's father marched on. Mrs. Twindlethorpe raised her broom, but she was too short to bean Wilmot's father on the head. She took aim and whacked him instead on his kilted buttocks.

Wilmot's father marched on. The pipes screamed. The dog leaped off its porch and galloped down the walkway, barking.

"Dad!" Wilmot shouted. "Come back!"

His words were lost in the wailing of the pipes, the barking of the dog and the yelling of old Mrs. Twindlethorpe.

At the edge of the dog's property, Wilmot's father stopped. The dog stood on the sidewalk, snarling. The music petered out. The snow fell gently. Wilmot tiptoed down the porch steps. Softly, he made his way toward his father. He would take his dad's arm and lead him home in an honorable retreat.

Just then, Dad straightened his shoulders. He blew another blast on the bagpipes.

The dog attacked. Its jaws closed on the red-and-green kilt. With a ripping sound, the kilt was torn from his father's body. Wilmot's worst fear was realized: his father was wearing the pink-smiley-face underwear. He grabbed his father's arm.

"Run, Dad! Run!" Together they sprinted through the snow, up the slippery stairs and through the front door, slamming it closed behind them.

"Barbarians!" Wilmot's father panted. He slid down to sit with his back against the door, his bare, hairy legs sticking out of his smiley-face underwear. "Neanderthals! Uncultured boors! The curse of the Balcanqualls upon all of them!"

The bagpipes hung limply in his arms. Wilmot touched the instrument. He felt the smooth wood of the pipes, the well-worn finger holes.

"Can I try it, Dad?"

"Can you try it?" said his father. "My son, it is your sacred duty to play these pipes!"

Wilmot tucked the bag under his arm. He put the mouthpiece between his lips. He blew. No sound came out. His lungs strained. He blew and blew again. A jumble of mangled notes blurted from the instrument.

"Needs tuning," his father muttered. He fiddled with the ivory knobs on the pipes.

Wilmot blew again. This time, the sound came out cleaner, and Wilmot felt a surge of unexpected joy—the powerful joy of making music. He blew again. Yes. He could see how, if he knew the fingering, he might be able to make a real note, a real melody.

The sound of the bagpipes filled the hallway—a buzz, a hum, a loud, raw, urgent call.

The call of music.

To Wilmot's ears, it sounded like the perfect music for Nocturnia, Vampire Princess of Doom.

TWENTY

Zombie Josh

Lucky thing Mom's working late tonight, Josh thought, as he stuck his finger in her creamy purple eye shadow and smeared it over the bump on his forehead. He rubbed some green eye shadow on the bruise around his right eye and leaned away from the mirror to admire the effect.

Gruesome.

Very gruesome.

"Eat brains!" Josh groaned in a throaty voice at his zombie reflection in the mirror. Wang and Magnolia were right. This opportunity to play a zombie was too good to pass up. After all, how often did a guy have a gory black eye *and* a swollen purple bump on his head at the same time? Once in his life—*if* he was lucky.

Besides not letting him use her makeup, Josh's mom (if she'd been home) would probably have asked him some awkward questions. Like, what the heck did he think he was doing, leaving the house at seven thirty on a Friday night dressed in his Fruit of the Loom long underwear beneath a tattered hoodie and a pair of ripped jeans?

"Eat brains," would have been Zombie-Josh's answer.

Somehow, he didn't think that answer would have gone over too well with his mom.

Turning away from his reflection, Josh zombie-walked out of the bathroom and into the front hall. He reached for his blue ski jacket in the front closet, put it on and checked himself out in the hall mirror. The jacket totally ruined the effect. He didn't look like a zombie. He looked like a klutzy kid who'd skied into a tree. Josh ditched the jacket and pulled on a black wool tuque. It wasn't that cold out. Besides, zombies were undead. They didn't need much body heat.

Outside, it was snowing—the steady kind of snow that could last all night, so that by morning the tree branches and rooftops and parked cars would all be covered in a thick layer of white. Looking up, he could see millions and millions of white specks against a dark gray sky—miles and miles of snowflakes, all the way up to the clouds.

Josh hugged himself and walked quickly to the park. Though it took up a whole block in a neighborhood of cozy red-brick houses, the park had no climbers or swing sets. Most of it was just a wide-open space where people walked their dogs and kids played soccer and Frisbee in the summer or threw snowballs in the winter. There was a hill on one side, marked by icy toboggan tracks, and a clump of winter-bare trees and bushes in the far corner. In the middle of the open space stood a single streetlamp, which cast a pinkish cone of light filled with steadily falling snowflakes.

Under the light stood the solitary figure of Headcase. They'd suggested the idea of an unvampiring ceremony to him, without revealing all the top-secret details, and he'd agreed to go along with it. The poor guy was so heartbroken, he'd do anything to get back together with his girlfriend.

Josh skirted the edge of the park and found Wang, Wilmot and Magnolia at their rendezvous point, crouched behind the clump of bushes.

"Hey, Josh," said Wilmot. "We were getting worried you'd never make it."

Wilmot was dressed as a piper, with thick wool socks, wool tartan kilt, wool sweater, wool scarf and wool beret. He had bagpipes tucked under his arm.

"I needed to add some extra face paint." Josh pointed to his gory black eye. "Like it?"

"Cool," said Wang, peeping out from beneath the lion's head. "Oh, by the way, I brought Zahraa along. I needed a rear end."

Zahraa gave a friendly wave with the lion's tail.

"Hi," said Josh.

"I'm the rear end," said Zahraa. "Please don't call me butthead."

"No," said Josh. "I never would."

Magnolia was wearing an ankle-length fur coat, a black fur hat and black gloves. She was also carrying a very cool scepter with a skull on top, which lit up and made thunder-and-lightning sounds when she pushed a button.

Josh looked longingly at her fur coat.

"Aren't you freezing to death?" said Magnolia.

"I can't freeze to death. I'm undead. Remember?" Josh said bravely.

"You're not really undead," Wilmot reminded him.

"I'm getting into character," said Josh.

"Your hands look frozen," said Wilmot.

"All zombies have frozen hands," said Josh. "It's because they're undead."

"And blue lips? You've got blue lips," said Wilmot. "Here, Josh. Take my scarf."

Wilmot unwound his long wool scarf and draped it around Josh's neck.

"Thanks," said Josh. The undead could wear a scarf. It could be part of The Look.

"Quiet!" whispered Magnolia. "Here she comes."

They peered out from the shrubbery. There, walking in a drifty, dreamy sort of way through the snow, came Headcase's ex-girlfriend, Freya. She was carrying a tall walking stick and wearing a long, shimmery, silver coat that swirled around her ankles. Magnolia waited until Freya stepped beneath the streetlamp. The cone of misty light, flecked with glittering snowflakes, formed an aura around her robed, silver form.

"Now!" whispered Magnolia.

A blast from Wilmot's bagpipes shattered the silence. The noble lion jumped out of the shrubbery. Nocturnia, Vampire Princess of Doom, emerged from the darkness as though rising from the grave. Josh, hoping it would all be over before he got frostbite, fell into place behind her. Slowly, Nocturnia's procession advanced across the lonely park.

Wang and Zahraa made the lion a high-kicking phantasm, a leaping, whirling rainbow of fluttering ribbons and glittering sequins that danced through the snow across the open field. Accompanying the lion came the raw bursts of sound from Wilmot's bagpipes. There was no tune or melody to these blasts of noise, yet they sounded powerful and somehow otherworldly, like the inarticulate cries of a homesick dragon. Behind Wilmot, with regal steps, walked Magnolia. The hem of her black robe brushed the white snow. Every few steps, she raised her scepter and sent red laser beams shooting out of the skull's eye sockets, along with the crackling sound of thunder.

Josh lurched along at the rear of the procession. As zombie slave, he considered it his duty to keep a lookout, and so, trying to ignore the snow soaking through his hoodie, he cast his one good eye around the landscape. On the sidewalk at the top of the toboggan hill, he glimpsed the shape of a person walking a dog. Apart from that, they had the park to themselves.

At last the procession reached the streetlamp. Wilmot's pipes fell silent. The Noble Lion settled into stillness. Magnolia stepped forward. She faced Headcase and raised her scepter.

"Behold, I am Nocturnia, Vampire Princess of Doom! Vampire Headcase, kneel before me!"

Headcase fell to one knee in the snow. Josh shivered in sympathy and stuffed his cold hands underneath his armpits.

"Vampire Headcase, you have displeased me!" Magnolia thundered.

Before she could continue, Freya stepped forward. The walking stick she carried was wreathed with feathers, dried leaves and berries, and she raised it aloft in a mirror image of Magnolia's skeleton scepter.

"Behold! I am Freya, Nymph of Love and Fertility!" she said. "I claim Headcase as my own. No longer shall he be subject to your evil powers!"

The two girls stared at each other. *This is an unexpected twist*, thought Josh. On the one hand, it seemed they'd accomplished their mission to get Freya and Headcase back together. On the other hand, you could never predict how Magnolia would handle an unexpected twist. She was, after all, an actress.

The snow sifted down. Magnolia and Freya glared at each other. Josh felt his blood crystallizing into ice inside his toes. Finally, Headcase rose from his knees, brushing the snow off his wet jeans.

"No offense, Your Vampireliness," he said to Magnolia. "But you heard what the love nymph said."

"Silence!" Magnolia stamped her foot and struck him with her scepter. "Kneel, minion! Do you think you can escape so easily from your dire Fate?"

Headcase eased himself back onto one knee.

Wilmot cast a worried look at Josh.

"What's she doing? What dire Fate?" he hissed. "I thought Freya and Headcase were *supposed* to get together."

"She's going off-script," muttered Josh.

"Not off-script!" moaned Wilmot.

"Silence, servants!" Magnolia shot red laser light at them from the skull scepter. "Or I shall turn you into octopuses!"

"Octopuses?" came the muffled voice of Wang from beneath the lion costume.

"Where'd she come up with that?" added Zahraa from the rear end.

But Josh was less worried about being turned into an octopus than he was about the dog walker, who had come down the toboggan hill and was now advancing toward them across the wide-open space of the park. Although he couldn't see well through his swollen eye and the falling snow, it seemed to Josh that there was something familiar about the person.

"Be gone, handmaiden of Darkness!" proclaimed Freya, pointing her staff at Magnolia. "Or I shall cast a spell to banish you to the gloomiest depths of Transylvania!"

"Insolent nymph!" Magnolia retorted. "Be gone yourself! Or *I* shall cast a spell to banish *you* to the frozen fjords of Iceland!"

"Indeed?" Freya shot back. "Well, *I* shall cast a spell to banish *you* to the wintry wasteland of Antarctica, where you will wander in desolation for a *thousand years!*"

"Never!" Magnolia cried. "For *I* shall cast a spell to banish *you* to the forsaken land of Dargron, where you will be tied to a cliff and the seven-headed hellhound Garbogra will feast upon your guts for a hundred millennia!"

"Not so!" Freya shouted. "For *I* shall cast a spell to banish *you* to the lifeless limits of the galaxy, where the interstellar forces of entropy shall shred your body into a million tiny pieces and send them spinning into outer space for *all eternity!*"

"Forsooth!" Magnolia yelled. "I shall cast a spell…"

But at that point Josh lost track of the spells. Because, squinting with his one good eye through the driving snow, he finally recognized the person coming toward them.

And he knew that if she reached them, she would ruin everything.

TWENTY-ONE

Unvampired

"Magnolia!" Josh nudged her urgently in the ribs.

"Silence! I am casting a spell!"

Magnolia raised her scepter.

Arganath, barganath, cranthren, krach,
Dragulan, bragulan, grangreth, grach!

"Oh, for Pete's sake!" Josh turned to Wilmot. "Wil, look over there. It's Stacey Hogarth."

"Stacey? What's she doing here?"

"I don't know, but she's going to ruin everything!"

It wasn't hard to imagine what Stacey would do if she got close enough to see what was happening. She'd shoot off her big mouth. She'd tell everyone that the Vampire Princess of Doom was really Magnolia, and that the lion was really Wang, and that Josh wasn't a zombie, just a freezing-cold kid in a snow-soaked hoodie. She'd destroy the magic of the moment, and then who knew if Freya and Headcase would ever get together?

"What are we gonna do?" whispered Wilmot.

"Create a distraction!" Wang hissed.

"What kind of distraction?"

"I know!" Josh broke in.

In a rasping voice, he moaned, "Eat brains!"

Josh turned away from the lamplight. He lurched toward Stacey. His teeth chattered. His fingers prickled with cold. His feet felt as heavy as blocks of ice. He was no longer Josh Johnson, mild-mannered school kid and president of Dunces Anonymous. He was Josh the zombie slave, on a mission to protect his mistress, Nocturnia, Vampire Princess of Doom, from the evil Enforcer Grrrrrl.

"Eat brains!" Zombie-Josh moaned even louder.

A burst of noise from Wilmot's bagpipes shattered the night air. Stacey's dog bounded toward Josh, barking.

"King! Come back here, King!" Stacey grabbed the dog's collar. "Who are you guys? What are you doing? Is that…is that Josh Johnson?"

"Eat brains!" Josh shuffled toward her.

"Josh? *Is* it Josh?" Stacey squinted at him through the snow. "Josh, come off it. This isn't funny. What are you doing?"

"EAT BRAINS!" Josh advanced toward her, his feet dragging through the snow.

Stacey stepped back.

The dog, a huge black Labrador, broke away from Stacey's grip, snarling.

Josh's zombie brain felt numb. Mindlessly, he repeated the zombie mantra: "EAT BRAINS!"

Hackles raised, the dog lunged forward. The Noble Lion jumped in front of Josh, blocking the dog's path. The lion's hind legs ballet-kicked the dog in the muzzle. The dog yelped and cringed back.

"EAT BRAINS!" Josh roared. Wilmot let out an earsplitting blast on the bagpipes. The dog turned tail and ran.

"King!" Stacey turned and ran after the dog. The Noble Lion chased them across the open field. They reached the base of the toboggan hill, lion and bagpiper in close pursuit. Slipping and stumbling, Stacey and her dog struggled up the slope, reached the sidewalk and sprinted out of sight. Panting, Josh caught up with the others at the bottom of the hill.

"You were awesome, Josh!" Wang slapped him on the back.

"Thanks," Josh said through chattering teeth. "Could I borrow your ski jacket? I think I'm dying of hypothermia."

"Anything for you, Prez," said Wang.

Josh pulled on Wang's ski jacket and instantly felt warmth flood into his body. With Stacey's disappearance, his zombie persona had slipped away and he was once again plain old Josh Johnson, an ordinary kid standing in long underwear and ripped jeans in the middle of a snow-covered park.

His feet felt dead numb.

"We should head home," he said.

"What about Headcase?" said Wilmot. "We don't even know if he's unvampired yet."

Josh looked back across the park. They'd come a long way from the streetlamp where Magnolia and Freya still stood in the cone of light, with Headcase on one knee between them.

"Ha! Your servants have deserted you! You are powerless against me!" came the voice of Freya in the distance.

"My servants shall return to me!" Magnolia shouted. "Servants, I command you to return!"

Josh looked at Wilmot. Wilmot looked at Wang. Wang looked at Zahraa.

"What do you guys think?" Josh asked.

"I'm cold," said Wang.

"My lungs hurt," said Wilmot.

"My mom said I could bring everyone home for hot chocolate," said Zahraa.

"Return to me!" Magnolia shouted.

"We're going for hot chocolate!" Josh shouted back.

"Ha! They obey your commands no longer!" Freya crowed. "Be gone to the darkness whence you came, vampire strumpet! Headcase is mine!"

Freya raised her arms in a swirl of silver cloak. Magnolia stumbled backward.

"Aaaaah! I am vanquished! My powers are fading!" Magnolia cried. "One last curse I set upon thee: may Headcase forever have webbed feet, as a symbol of the vampire he once was!"

Magnolia staggered out of the cone of light. She reeled across the snow-covered ground and exited, stage left, into the shrubbery.

"Guess we should go catch up with her," said Josh. The others nodded.

They made their way across the frozen park, retracing their footprints through the snow. The bagpipes were silent now. The lion no longer danced. The trek back seemed farther, their steps slower. It felt like the end of a parade, the enchantment fading, the world returning to its everyday self. Yet in the misty light of the streetlamp, a scene was still playing out between Freya and Headcase. Bending toward him in her flowing robe, she reached down her hand and lifted him to his feet. Rising, he clasped her in his arms.

"Don't look now!" groaned Wang. "They're smooching!"

It was true. They were smooching. But as Josh and his friends passed by, just outside the halo of lamplight, Headcase unclenched one arm from his girlfriend's waist. He raised his hand and flashed them the universal symbol of rock 'n' roll.

TWENTY-TWO

Holding the Drones

Wilmot couldn't sleep. The moonlight flowing through his window rubbed against the dark wood of his bagpipe case and polished it to a shine. Wilmot lay in bed, staring at it. The only sound was the ticking of the grandfather clock in the downstairs hallway. The only light, besides the glowing red 12:05 on his clock radio, was the shaft of moonlight falling on his bagpipe case.

Three days until the concert. He was worried about the bagpipes.

Everything else in their plan was coming together. Headcase had promised to play lead guitar at the hockey game. "I owe you, little dudes," he'd said. Wang was getting the hang of the drums. Magnolia, though still technically grounded, had convinced her mom to let her go to band practice because she needed the musical training for her future career as an actress. Dressed in character as a rocker chick, she was learning to belt out the vocals for their hard-wailing, chord-busting "Rock Anthem to Principal Hale."

Only Wilmot still struggled with his instrument.

It was one thing to blurt out blasts of sound to scare off Stacey Hogarth's dog in a deserted park. It was a totally different thing to play the bagpipes properly. If Wilmot was going to stand in an arena in front of hundreds of screaming schoolkids and play the bagpipes to "Rock Anthem to Principal Hale," he wanted to play them properly.

To do that, he needed to hold the drones.

The three big pipes that stuck out the top of the bag were called the drones. If he could play the bagpipes properly, the air in the bag would flow through the drones, creating a long-drawn-out thrumming sound, harmonious and melancholic, that never faded but went on and on. Above the thrumming of the drones, he would play his melody on the chanter—the small pipe at the bottom of the bag, drilled with finger holes like a flute—and it would sound like birdsong rising above the hum of cicadas on a hot summer's day.

But he had to learn to hold the drones.

To hold the drones, he had to blow enough air into the bag so that the sound never wavered, never stuttered or failed. Try as he might, Wilmot couldn't get the hang of it. His father had been trying to teach him ever since he'd given him the bagpipes nearly three weeks ago. As soon as Wilmot got home from school, his father, instead of presenting him with chess puzzles, would send him up to his room to change into his full piper's regalia: kilt, wool socks, dress shirt, tie and piper's cap. They'd meet in the living room for practice.

"Shoulders back! Spine straight! Head high! Deep breath! Now attack the pipes! Attack!" his dad would command.

Wilmot felt like the pipes were attacking him.

He knew the bag was supposed to stay tucked under his arm, but it squirmed and wriggled like Baby Garland in his stroller. As soon as Wilmot got a grasp on the bag, the drones would flop and flail around. Even if he did manage to get a grip on the instrument, blowing air into the bag was another problem. The bag was made of sheepskin, and blowing it up felt like trying to inflate an oversized leather soccer ball using a soda straw.

"Breathe deeper! Deeper!" his dad would urge him.

But Wilmot's breath didn't go any deeper. He felt as though he'd need lungs the size of an elephant to blow up the bag and keep it inflated. Instead of the steady thrumming of the drones, his bagpipes produced only random blurts of sound, like a herd of sheep with indigestion burping on a Scottish hillside.

"Attack the pipes! Attack the pipes!" his dad would insist.

Under his father's eyes, Wilmot would break into a sweat. His hands would grow slippery. Moisture would soak the headband of his cap. Beads of sweat would trickle down his neck in a tickly, itchy, uncomfortable way that made him squirm. He'd forget to blow, and the bag would deflate with the whine of a punctured accordion until the instrument rested in his arms, a limp jumble of wooden pipes.

At last his father would throw up his hands in despair. "You'll never be a piper!"

I will be a piper, Wilmot thought, as he watched the red numbers on his clock radio turn to 12:06. *I will.*

Wilmot slipped out from under the covers. His feet tingled on the cold wood floor. He crossed the room, unlocked the latches on the bagpipe case and opened it. The smell of leather and grease wafted out. A shiver ran through him. It reminded him of the times he'd gotten up in the middle of the night to play his guitar, slipping the cardboard sweater box out from under his bed and opening it to find those red thunderbolts winking at him.

Wilmot put the thought out of his head. He must not think of the guitar. The pipes were his instrument now—brought across the Atlantic Ocean from Scotland by his great-great-great-grandfather, Angus Balcanquall, at the age of just sixteen. Wilmot tried to imagine what it would feel like for a boy only five years older than himself to leave his home and his country and travel to a new land where he had no friends, carrying nothing but the clothes on his back and the bagpipes under his arm. Those bagpipes lay before him now in their old wooden box, lit by the same moon that had lit the journey of Angus Balcanquall.

"I *will* be a piper," Wilmot whispered.

He took a deep breath. The cold air sharpened his senses. He lifted the bagpipes from the box.

Attack the pipes.

He took a breath so deep his lungs and stomach ached. He blew. He inhaled and blew again. The bag puffed up like a balloon. Wilmot gave it two sharp taps, as his father had shown him, and tucked it under his arm. Head up. Shoulders back. Spine straight. He took a breath so deep it seemed to fill his entire body, then blew.

A sound came forth—a reedy hum of many-layered notes. It wavered, started to drop, like a tiny bird falling from its nest, but Wilmot caught it and lifted it up with another puff of air. He felt his lungs working in a rhythm of inhale and exhale, a rhythm that kept the bag swollen with air, a rhythm that sustained the notes.

The music grew in strength. It filled the four walls of Wilmot's bedroom. It swelled like a bubble about to burst. Only it didn't burst. It kept on swelling, until it felt to Wilmot as though the music was not only around him, but inside him. As though he had dissolved into the music. As though the bagpipes were part of his body, or his body was part of the bagpipes— he didn't know which, and he didn't care. The sound went on and on. The thrumming of the drones. The half-brave, half-sad music of the bagpipes.

Caught up in the spell, Wilmot didn't hear the thudding of footsteps in the hallway. He didn't know that anyone else was awake until the door to his room flew open and his father appeared, in red-striped pajamas and with his black hair sticking up at all angles from his head, shouting, "Wilmot Binkle! What in the name of—?"

His father stopped. He stared. His mouth hung agape.

"Wilmot! By gad! You're holding the drones!"

Wilmot didn't dare take the blowstick out of his mouth, in case the musical charm was broken. He nodded—inhaling, exhaling. His father drew up his shoulders. He flung back his head. He sang loudly in an imitation Scottish accent:

Over the lochs
Blooms the bonny, bonny phlox!
Where my darling fair lass is a-waiting…

Wilmot's mother stumbled into the room. Her fuzzy bathrobe hung crookedly around her shoulders. Her hair looked like someone had scribbled it onto her head.

"It's very late at night," she said in a hoarse voice, squinting at them.

"Do you hear him, Ellen?" Wilmot's father shouted. "He's holding the drones! By gad! My son! My son is holding the drones!"

"Lovely, dear," his mom croaked. "Do you think we could all go back to bed now?"

Wilmot looked at his father. His father nodded. Wilmot took the blowstick out of his mouth and let the sound of the pipes fade. But though the sound faded, the feeling stayed with him.

"Sorry, Mom. I just…"

"That's all right, Wilmot. Maybe you could play again for me in the morning."

"Sure, Mom."

He laid the pipes in their box and closed the lid. But before he turned to go to bed, he felt his father lay a hand on his shoulder.

"Well done, Wilmot, lad," he said. "We'll make a piper out of you yet."

TWENTY-THREE

Rock On, Principal Hale

Clutching his bagpipes under his arm, Wilmot peeked around the corner of the concrete hallway, into the hockey arena full of screaming fans. It was so cold he could see his breath. So cold the noises ricocheted off the frozen metal rafters like pucks pinging off a goalpost—the shouts of the crowd, the whistle of the ref, the scrape of skate blades on the ice, the crunch of players hitting the boards. Two minutes left to play in the first period of the Principal's Challenge Cup.

Two minutes till showtime.

The score was 4-1 Oakview. The game was rough and scrappy, both on the ice and in the stands. The students had been given the afternoon off school to attend, and the seats were packed. Five hundred kids dressed in the green of the Oakview Overachievers faced off against five hundred fans wearing the blue of the Kilborn Killers, whose motto was Born to Kill.

Earlier in the period, things had gotten out of hand when a Killers fan dumped his extra-large buttered popcorn down the shirt of an Oakview girl. The girl fought back by smushing her ketchup-covered hamburger into the Kilborn kid's face, and the arena erupted into a massive food fight that only ended when the teachers hauled the worst offenders out of the stands and shut down the snack bar so no one could go back to replenish their ammo.

"What if they throw stuff at us?" Wilmot worried.

"Chill, little dude," said Headcase, guitar slung across his hips. "We're gonna rock."

The corridor where they stood led to a roped-off seating section opposite the Oakview bench. For the first period of the game, the section had remained empty except for Wang's drum kit, Magnolia's microphone and Headcase's amplifier. Freya—who happened to be the stage manager in her high school's drama club—had set up spotlights in the arena rafters. Now she sat in the glassed-off announcer's booth on the opposite side of the stands, ready to light the show.

Thirty seconds left in the period. Wilmot puffed up his bagpipes and wiped his sweaty hands on his kilt. He hoped he was wearing the right outfit for a rock 'n' roll bagpiper: worn-out gym shoes, kilt and a Metallica concert T-shirt that he'd borrowed from Headcase. Wang, wearing ordinary jeans and a T-shirt, was tapping his drumsticks hyperactively against the concrete wall of the hallway. Magnolia, dressed in a shiny silver top, leather jacket, leather pants and silver platform boots, was pacing up and down, muttering the lyrics to "Rock Anthem to Principal Hale" under her breath. Only Headcase didn't seem nervous. Lounging against the wall with his shaggy hair half covering his eyes, picking lazily on his guitar, he looked like an authentic rock 'n' roll star.

Ten seconds left in the period. The arena full of fans shouted the countdown. Nine, eight, seven, six, five, four, three, two, one...

AAAAAAANNNNNGGGGHHHHHH!

The buzzer sounded.

Showtime.

The lights in the arena went out. The noise of the crowd fell to a mumble.

"You ready, little dudes?" said Headcase.

"Ready," said Wang and Magnolia.

"Ready," said Wilmot. He put the blowstick into his mouth.

"All right," said Headcase. "Let's rock!"

His hand brushing against the cold concrete wall, Wilmot felt his way along the hallway into the roped-off section of the stands. The oval ice surface glowed white at the bottom of the arena, but the crowd appeared as nothing more than a mass of shadows, whispering, rustling, shuffling. Wilmot groped his way up the concrete steps and slid into place between the benches.

In the row below, he could see the shadowy outline of Wang's drum kit as Wang slipped into place. He heard him rap the steel rim of the snare drum with a drumstick, heard the click and the whine of feedback as Headcase plugged his guitar into its amp, heard the *tap-tap* of Magnolia testing her microphone. There was silence for the space of a breath. Then light burst into Wilmot's face, and Magnolia, who looked like a black cut-out against the blinding white glare, shouted into her microphone, "HOCKEY FANS, DO YOU WANNA ROCK?"

The opening guitar chord ripped through the arena. A thousand hyped-up kids screamed, "YAAAAAAAAH!"

Breathe, Wilmot told himself. *Just breathe.*

He breathed. He blew. The cry of the bagpipes filled the air—soft, then loud, then louder. The hum of the drones grew and swelled until it formed a solid wall of sound all around him, and the other sounds crashed against it like ocean waves crashing against a rocky cliff—the roar of the crowd, the chords of Headcase's guitar, the beat of Wang's drums, and Magnolia's voice as she began belting out "Rock Anthem to Principal Hale."

Five, four, three, two, one...

AAAAAAANNNNNGGGGHHHHHH!

The buzzer sounded. Josh skated to the players' bench and grabbed a seat next to Principal Hale.

Josh was feeling great. His black eye was healed, and he'd managed to survive the first period without injury. He'd even passed the puck to Stacey, who had scored a goal on his assist. If he and Stacey could work together on the same team, nothing was impossible.

Josh looked across at the roped-off seating section, where the drums and amplifier stood, waiting for the band to play. Soon it would be the moment of truth— the moment when their cunning plan either scored brilliantly or collapsed in a heap, cross-checked by the cruel forces of fate.

"Shouldn't we go to the dressing room, sir?" one of the players leaned over and asked.

"Not with a 4-1 lead!" Principal Hale crossed his arms over his chest. "Let's sit back and enjoy the show!"

The arena lights blacked out. Silence fell. The stage lights flashed on, accompanied by the wail of Headcase's guitar. Magnolia, dressed like a rocker chick, appeared in the dazzling glare of the spotlight. She pumped her fist at the crowd.

"HOCKEY FANS, DO YOU WANNA ROCK?"

"YAAAAAAAAH!" The scream went up all around him.

Principal Hale slammed his hands over his ears. He turned to Josh.

"I thought this was a country band!" he shouted.

"Don't worry, sir!" Josh shouted back. "You're gonna love them!"

I hope, he added under his breath. But there was no time to contemplate the possibility of failure, as Magnolia's voice soared through the icy rafters.

Who rocks?
Principal Hale!

Gonna win the game
Gonna never fail!
Hale, Hale, rock on!
Hale, Hale, rock on!
Who rocks?
Principal Hale!
Like a brave knight
In a fairy tale!
Hale, Hale, rock on!
Hale, Hale, rock on!

Magnolia held out her microphone. All around Josh, the hockey players banged their sticks against the boards in time to the beat. A thousand voices in the stands chanted, *"Hale, Hale, rock on! Hale, Hale, rock on!"*

Principal Hale unclenched his hands from his ears.

"Hey, this isn't too bad!" he shouted.

"I told you, sir!" Josh shouted back. He banged his stick and repeated the chorus: *"Hale, Hale, rock on! Hale, Hale, rock on!"*

Magnolia spun around. She thrust her fist in the air.

Who rocks?
Principal Hale!
Rock him on down

Crying hail to Hale!
Hale, Hale, rock on!
Hale, Hale, rock on!

Headcase jumped onto the railing that separated the tiers of benches. The crowd screamed. The white light silhouetted his skinny body and the curved shape of his guitar. He shook his long hair and let loose a torrent of notes that climbed higher and higher up the scale, building to a final cry that hung in the air until it was drowned out by the shrieks of the crowd.

Headcase jumped off the railing.

"Who rocks?" Magnolia shouted.

"Principal Hale!" the crowd shouted back.

"Tell me, who rocks?" shouted Magnolia.

"Principal Hale!"

"Louder! Who rocks?"

"Principal Hale!"

"Hale! Hale! Principal Hale!"

"Rock him on down, gonna—"

Ffsst! Eeeeeeeeeeeeeee! Grhnk!!!!

The music came screeching to a halt. The stage lights blinked off, plunging the arena into darkness. Confused cries of complaint rose from the crowd.

The pale, fluorescent arena lights flickered on, and a voice came over the PA system.

"May I have your attention, please, boys and girls! This is Belinda Hogarth, the head of the Oakview School Parent Council!"

"Belinda Hogarth!" Principal Hale leaped from the bench. "What does she think she's doing? That was my song! She cut off my song!"

"Yeah, she cut off his song!" shouted some of the players on the bench.

Russell, the hefty defenseman, jumped to his feet. "You want me to take her down, sir?"

Principal Hale put a hand on his shoulder. "No, son. No need to get into a brawl."

"As you may know"—Belinda Hogarth's voice filled the stadium over the crackly PA system—"the rental of this arena was paid for by the school's Junior Hockey budget. Furthermore, Section 34-C of the Oakview School Official Rule Book states that only participants in officially sanctioned school activities may perform at any school-sponsored event. I regret to inform you that, since the school's Drama and Music Program was unfortunately canceled due to circumstances beyond our control, this musical performance is *not* authorized. Therefore, I shall have to ask the band to leave the premises, immediately and forthwith. Luckily, my daughter's Spirit Committee has put together an exciting show for you…"

The boos of the crowd drowned out the voice on the PA system. Two of the girls on the team cornered Stacey and started yelling at her. Stacey stood up and yelled back at them. Some girls dressed in sequined figure-skating outfits skated onto the ice. Josh looked on, aghast, as kids from the crowd started picking up the leftovers from the food fight and pelting the girls with soggy French fries.

"What is the meaning of this? WHAT IS THE MEANING OF THIS?" Principal Hale roared. His jowls quivered. "I'd like to know who's the boss of this school, me or Belinda Hogarth?"

"You are, sir!" Josh piped up.

"That's right! I am!"

"Don't let her get away with it, sir!" Josh urged.

"I won't! By golly, I won't!" Principal Hale fumed.

He barged past the players on the bench and pounded up the steps two at a time toward the announcer's booth. Craning his neck, Josh saw him disappear through the glass doorway.

Fffsst! Eeeeeeeeeeeeeee! Grhnk!!!!

The music came screeching to a halt. The stage lights blinked off, plunging the arena into darkness.

Wilmot let the blowstick drop from his mouth. The sound of the bagpipes fizzled to a deflated wheeze. He looked around, squinting. What was going on? Had they blown a fuse in the electrical system? Could Freya fix it? How could this happen, just when the show was going so well? The pale, fluorescent arena lights flickered on, and a voice came over the PA system:

"May I have your attention, please, boys and girls! This is Belinda Hogarth, the head of the Oakview School Parent Council!"

"Stacey Hogarth's mother!" Magnolia gasped.

"What's she doing?" cried Wilmot.

He looked around frantically, trying to locate Mrs. Hogarth, but black spots patterned the air before his eyes. He seemed to see a phantom silhouette of Headcase, rocking out on his guitar, drift toward the arena rafters. At last, squinting at the glassed-in announcer's booth, Wilmot could just make out the figure of a person holding a microphone.

Numb with shock and cold, the buzz of phantom music still in his ears, Wilmot could barely hear what Mrs. Hogarth was saying. Something about the rules, and the band leaving the premises. Then scraps of food started flying—cold popcorn coated with congealed yellowish grease, hot-dog buns soaked with a rainbow of ketchup, mustard and relish…

"I knew they were going to throw stuff at us!" Wilmot cried.

"Chill, little dude." Wilmot felt Headcase's hand on his shoulder. "Don't panic."

But Wilmot could feel himself panicking, his throat tightening, his chest constricting, his forehead breaking into a sweat. He was turning to make a run for the exit when a man's voice boomed through the PA system.

"ATTENTION, STUDENTS! THIS IS PRINCIPAL HALE! SIT DOWN, SHUT YOUR MOUTHS AND STOP WHATEVER YOU'RE DOING!"

The noise in the arena fell to a murmur. A final French fry flew in a ketchuppy arc toward the rink and splatted onto the ice. Wilmot turned back toward the band.

"I SAW THAT, TIMMY BUTLER! AND I'LL SEE YOU IN MY OFFICE FIRST THING TOMORROW MORNING! ANY OTHER SMART ALECKS OUT THERE?"

The principal's voice echoed around the rafters. No one in the audience budged. Wilmot looked around. The arena was perfectly still and silent.

"GOOD! THEN LISTEN UP!" the principal said. "I INVITED THE BAND TO PERFORM TODAY, AND I THINK THEY'VE DONE A MIGHTY FINE JOB. YESSIR, MIGHTY FINE! IN FACT, I THINK THEY DESERVE A ROUND OF APPLAUSE!"

A few kids started clapping. Then more. Then more. The clapping turned into boot-stomping. The boot-stomping turned into cheering. The cheering turned into screaming. And the screaming rattled the rafters. Headcase jumped onto the railing and raised his hand in the symbol of rock 'n' roll. The crowd went crazy. Wilmot hugged his bagpipes. He felt himself smiling and a blush rising to his cheeks. Wang turned to him, grinning, and flashed a thumbs-up sign. As the noise of the crowd died down, the principal's voice came over the loudspeakers again.

"BEFORE TODAY, I WAS A COUNTRY MUSIC FAN THROUGH AND THROUGH. BUT THE TALENT OF THESE GIFTED YOUNG MUSICIANS HAS OPENED MY EYES TO THE POWER OF ROCK AND ROLL! YES. IT'S TRUE THAT THE SCHOOL'S DRAMA AND MUSIC PROGRAM WAS CANCELED DUE TO—AHEM—THE PRESSURE OF BUDGETARY PRIORITIES. BUT I ASK YOU STUDENTS: CAN

DOLLARS AND CENTS QUELL THE PASSION OF MUSIC? CAN MERE MONEY QUASH THE SPIRIT OF ROCK AND ROLL? LET ME HEAR YOU SAY NO!"

"NO!" shouted the crowd.

"LET ME HEAR IT LOUDER!"

"NO!"

"RIGHT!" shouted Principal Hale. "AND I AM HERE TO TELL YOU THAT FROM THIS MOMENT FORWARD, THE DRAMA AND MUSIC PROGRAM IS BACK ON AT OAKVIEW SCHOOL!"

Screams erupted from the crowd. Magnolia squealed and jumped up and down. Wang threw Wilmot a high five.

"FURTHERMORE," the principal continued, "IN ORDER TO ALLOW MRS. KARLOFF TO TEACH DRAMA AND MUSIC, I MYSELF WILL BE TAKING OVER THE JUNIOR FRENCH CLASSES FOR THE REST OF THE SEMESTER!

"AND SO, MES AMIS, I SAY TO YOU, VIVE LE HOCKEY! VIVE LE DRAMA AND MUSIC PROGRAM! AND, MOST OF ALL, VIVE LE ROCK AND ROLL!"

With a whine and a screech, Headcase's amplifier shot back to life. Headcase pealed out a chord that rang to the rafters.

Magnolia grabbed her microphone and shouted: "WHO ROCKS?"

"PRINCIPAL HALE!" the crowd shouted back.

Wang laid down a beat on the drums. Wilmot took a deep breath and struck up the skirl of the bagpipes.

The rest of the concert was a blur of sound and light. It seemed to Wilmot that no time had passed before the buzzer sounded, calling the hockey players back onto the ice. The spotlights went off. The arena lighting blinked on. And still the crowd cheered. Wilmot looked out over the faces in the audience, hundreds of cheering faces—kids, teachers, parents.

Wait…parents…

He scanned the arena more closely.

Two figures stood in a doorway in the far corner. One was short, plump and wearing a long coat. The other was tall, thin, with—yes—a dark beard.

Parents.

Not just any parents.

His parents.

Wilmot, face flushed, heart hammering, stared at them from across the arena, and it was as though he were looking through a telescope, seeing only them, shutting out everything else in the building.

Dunces Rock

His parents had come to hear him play.

And, to Wilmot's amazement, they were holding their hands high and applauding.

TWENTY-FOUR

The Bonny, Bonny Phlox

Wilmot hadn't been thinking much about his birthday that year. What with the guitar, and the bagpipes, and the concert, and the unvampiring, there had just been too many things to think about. But it came around, like his birthday always did, on March 17, the Saturday after the concert.

Wilmot usually celebrated his birthday with just his mom and dad, and maybe his grandparents, if they made it into town for the occasion. But this time, he invited Wang and Josh and Magnolia and Zahraa. He invited Headcase too, but the teenager had to go to work at the grocery warehouse. "Sorry, little dude. The tinned beans need me," he'd said. But he'd presented Wilmot with a new guitar pick and a set of strings, wrapped in a page torn from *Guitar World* magazine.

Even without Headcase, it was still Wilmot's best birthday ever. First they went tobogganing at the park where they'd performed the unvampiring ceremony. When their pants were soaked through, they went back to Wilmot's place, where his mom ordered pizza and they watched one of Wang's Kung Fu movies in the basement rec room. Wang tried to teach them the trick of walking up the wall and flipping over, but no one else could master it.

"That was the coolest move ever, Wang," said Zahraa, sitting cross-legged on the floor and biting into a slice of pepperoni pizza. "You should've won the audition for sure."

"You were really good too," said Wang.

"Oh, well." Zahraa shrugged. "Larry. What a fake."

"Yeah," said Wang. "But you know what? Who cares? We got to dance the lion dance anyway, right? And it was way more fun scaring off Stacey."

"In a way, it all worked out," Zahraa agreed.

Wang pulled a slice of gooey four-cheese pizza out of the box, wrapping strings of mozzarella around his fingers.

"*And* we got the Drama and Music program back," added Magnolia. "Which means I get to audition for *Nocturnia, Vampire Princess of Doom*."

"*And* you guys played an awesome concert at the hockey game," said Josh. "Especially Wil."

"Yeah, Wil," said Wang. "You were amazing. I didn't even know you could play rock music on the bagpipes."

"Thanks," said Wil. He bit into the crust of his pizza and smiled at his friends, remembering how it had felt to stand in the noisy arena, surrounded by his bandmates in that circle of light that set them apart from the crowd—to feel the music swelling through him, through the bagpipes, through the air all around him. It was a beautiful feeling. Beautiful, and a little sad. The way the sound of the pipes itself was a little sad, always calling for something missing.

Something missing.

His guitar.

He stifled the thought and reached for another piece of pizza. He wouldn't let sad thoughts ruin his perfect birthday.

"Cake and presents, kids!" Wilmot's mom called.

They thundered upstairs and grabbed seats around the dining-room table. His mom had laid out a white tablecloth and her best dishes—even the little silver forks that she kept for special occasions. Next to Wilmot's plate sat a large silver cake knife. Wilmot's dad sat in a chair in the corner of the dining room. His dad hated noisy parties with lots of kids, and though he wasn't smiling or talking, at least he was there. Wilmot gave him a little smile as his mom dimmed the lights and hurried into the kitchen. She started singing the happy-birthday song, and his friends joined in as she came through the kitchen door, carrying a huge chocolate cake alight with eleven candles.

The cake sat glowing in front of Wilmot.

"Make a wish!" his mom said.

He closed his eyes and thought about what to wish for. He had everything he wanted. Everything, except maybe one thing. He knew he'd never get it back, but still…it couldn't hurt to wish for it.

He blew out the candles in a single breath.

"I call first piece!" shouted Wang.

"Wang! That's rude!" said Magnolia.

"That's okay," said Wilmot. He picked up the silver cake knife and cut a huge piece for Wang. He cut two pieces with icing flowers for Magnolia and Zahraa. He and Josh got ordinary pieces, but they shared licking the icing off the stubs of the birthday candles. In no time, their plates were empty except for crumbs.

His mom cleared off the plates and piled a heap of brightly wrapped birthday presents onto a chair beside Wilmot. She gave him a mysterious wink, disappeared into the kitchen again and returned carrying a large, flat box. It was at least twice as big as any other present, wrapped in silver-and-black paper with a huge silver bow on top. She placed it on the table in front of Wilmot.

"What's this, Mom?"

"Something special." She smiled. "Open it."

Wilmot unstuck the tape from the neatly folded end of the wrapping paper. Normally, he just ripped presents open. But this paper was so thick, the silver so shiny, the black so velvety, that it seemed wrong to tear it. He turned the box over and ran his finger under the slit where the wrapping paper overlapped, unsticking the bits of tape. From beneath the wrapping paper emerged a plain brown cardboard box. He looked up. His mother smiled. His father leaned forward in his chair. Wilmot fit his fingers under the cardboard lid and wiggled it up, gently, inch by inch, until it came off with a little sigh of suctioned air. He pushed the lid aside. He looked in the box.

His heart nearly stopped beating.

"Mom?" He gasped. "Mom!"

He jumped from his chair and threw his arms around her.

"I can't believe you got it back!"

"I just thought…"

"I love it! I love you!" Wilmot squeezed his mother tightly. He let her go and reached out to touch the shiny, black paint, the shimmering strings, the red thunderbolts…

"That *thing*." His father rose from his seat. "What is that *thing* doing in my house?"

"Now, dear"—his mother stepped between them—"it's Wilmot's birthday."

"But that *thing*! How did it get here?"

"I went back and got it the next day from the thrift shop. Now, don't get upset. I was thinking, you know, that it *did* belong to Wilmot. I was thinking that we'd made a mistake."

"A mistake?" his father repeated. "A mistake?" A flush rose in his face. He gripped the table.

"In giving away something that belonged to Wilmot," his mom explained. "Something that wasn't ours to take."

"That wasn't ours…" His father looked around the room. He was red in the face. Wilmot's friends sat motionless, gaping at him.

He turned to the window, pulling himself together.

"Dad," said Wilmot.

His father didn't answer. Wilmot looked back and forth between the guitar, so shiny in its nest of silver wrapping paper, and his father's back, so rigidly set against him.

"Dad, please," said Wilmot.

"I thought," came his father's choked voice, "I thought you were a piper, son."

"But I am, Dad! I *am* a piper! It's just that…"

"It's just that I begged him to learn the guitar!" Magnolia exclaimed, jumping out of her chair. "Not for his own sake, but for mine! Oh, sir! Please forgive your kindhearted son!"

Magnolia fell to her knees beside his dad. Wilmot stared at her, astounded.

"You?" His father peered down at her. "Who are you?"

"My name is Magnolia, sir."

"And what have you got to do with this…this… instrument?"

"Alas, sir! I urged Wilmot to take this cast-off guitar and learn to play it, so that he could accompany my singing at the school talent show. It was just a simple song, an old Scottish ballad that my dear old grandmother used to sing as she bounced me on her knee…"

"An old Scottish ballad?"

"Yes, sir. It was called 'Over the Lochs'—"

"'Blooms the Bonny, Bonny Phlox,'" his father interrupted. "I know it, of course! And do you mean to tell me that Wilmot can play that tune upon this guitar?"

He turned to Wilmot.

"Can you, Wilmot?"

His father's eyes were dark and stern, his brow furrowed, his jaw clenched. But Wilmot didn't feel afraid. Not even nervous. He felt strangely happy.

He lifted the guitar from the box. He fit the strap over his shoulder. He plucked the strings and turned the tuning pegs until the vibrating notes hit the sweet spot. He strummed a C chord.

"If you could hum a few bars," he said to his dad.

His dad raised his eyebrows in surprise. He cleared his throat. "Well, I suppose…" He began to hum. It was an easy chord progression—D, B minor, E minor, G. Wilmot added a simple picking pattern. His father raised his voice and sang:

Over the lochs
Blooms the bonny, bonny phlox,

Where my darling fair lass is a-waiting!
I shall cross hill and dell
For the one I love so well,
Though the light of the day is a-fading!

His father held the last note, letting it gradually die out. He turned to Wilmot. He smiled.

"That was…musical," he said.

"It was wonderful!" Wilmot's mom exclaimed.

"So you'll let me keep it, Dad?" said Wilmot. "You'll let me play it?"

"I…well…you won't abandon the pipes, will you, Wilmot?"

"Never, Dad! I'll play them both!"

"You must practice every day!"

"Yes, Dad."

"I'll get you a proper teacher."

"Sure, Dad."

"You may have to give up the chess club…"

"I could do that, Dad."

"…to devote yourself to your music."

"That's all I want, Dad! To devote myself to my music!"

"Well, then, in good conscience, Wilmot, I don't see how I could say no."

Wilmot let out a yelp, slung back his guitar and flung his arms around his father. His dad's beard prickled against the skin of his forehead. *I'll need an amplifier,* Wilmot thought, his mind whirling. *I bet Headcase would give me his old one. I could set it up in the rec room. No one does anything down there but watch TV. And a couple of cool distortion pedals and—*

But one thing at a time. He had his guitar. He had his bagpipes. That was already a lot to be thankful for. Looking around at his friends and family, Wilmot suddenly felt as though everything he was, and everything he would become, was contained in those two instruments.

The guitar for adventure. The pipes for tradition.

The danger of the red thunderbolts. The comfort of the well-worn wood.

The hard-driving riff that urged him forward.

The note through the fog that called him home.

Acknowledgments

If this book had never been written, Wilmot Binkle would have been stranded at the end of *Dunces Anonymous* without ever learning how to play the electric guitar. Wilmot and I therefore owe many people our thanks for making this book happen.

Thank you to Mark Baker, who came up with the original idea for *Dunces Anonymous*, and to all my writing colleagues who offered advice and encouragement. Thank you to my daughter Zoey, who commanded me to write a sequel, and to my daughter Molly, who made sure the second book included Baby Garland.

Thank you to the folks at the Ottawa Folklore Centre for letting me use their studio to shoot the book trailer, and especially to Ross Davison, for the bagpipe lesson. Thank you to Tony Fan and Vitus So of Success Lion Dance for sharing their knowledge of the lion dance with me and inviting me to watch one of their beautiful performances.

Thank you to everyone involved in the book trailer: lead guitarist Noah (Wilmot), Zoey (Nocturnia, Vampire Princess of Doom), Sam (Josh), Molly (Baby Garland), Josh (Wang), Katherine (Stacey) and John (Mr. Binkle). Thank you to Agnes, Stuart and Matthew for letting me use their house and drum set. Thank you to John Bainbridge for creating the *Dunces Rock* doodle-art poster.

Thank you to my husband, Mark, for everything.

And, of course, thank you to Orca Book Publishers and my editor, Sarah Harvey, for having enough confidence in this gang of Dunces to publish a sequel.

Kate Jaimet developed an early taste for madcap plotlines due to childhood exposure to the novels of P.G. Wodehouse. Her batty characters are mainly based upon members of her own family. Kate enjoys limericks, yoga, clever repartee, kayaking and spending time with her two young daughters. Visit her website at www.katejaimet.com.